HAWK AGAINST CAT

Hawk heard his woman Raven Eyes gasp, whirled and saw her looking at the giant cougar crouching on a rock shelf just above him. Dropping to one knee, Hawk swung up his rifle. The cat was in mid-air when Hawk pulled the trigger. Off balance when he fired, the rifle's powerful recoil knocked him flat. The cat took the bullet in his right shoulder, slammed down onto Hawk, his claws digging into Hawk's neck and chest, the crushing force of the cougar's muscled body grinding Hawk into the ledge. Hawk felt the cat's great weight on his chest and felt the sickening snap as one of this ribs gave way. Poised on Hawk, with a right shoulder streaming from the bullet wound, the cat turned his head and looked deep into Hawk's eyes. Then the cat snarled, uttering a cry so filled with savage fury its roar seemed to fill the universe . . .

THE
EYES OF
THE CAT

THE EYES OF THE CAT

Will C. Knott

A SIGNET BOOK

NEW AMERICAN LIBRARY

PUBLISHER'S NOTE

This book is a work of fiction. Names, characters, places, and incidents either are the product of the author's imagination or are used fictitiously, and any resemblance to actual persons, living or dead, events, or locales is entirely coincidental.

Copyright © 1988 by Will C. Knott

All rights reserved

SIGNET TRADEMARK REG. U.S. PAT. OFF. AND FOREIGN COUNTRIES
REGISTERED TRADEMARK—MARCA REGISTRADA
HECHO EN CHICAGO, U.S.A.

SIGNET, SIGNET CLASSIC, MENTOR, ONYX, PLUME, MERIDIAN and NAL BOOKS are published by NAL PENGUIN INC., 1633 Broadway, New York, New York 10019

First Printing, March, 1988

1 2 3 4 5 6 7 8 9

PRINTED IN THE UNITED STATES OF AMERICA

—1—

It was close to sundown when Hawk heard the cat the first time. A big male. Close by. Too damn close. Possibly on the timbered ridge above the cabin. Something in the cat's snarl—a fierce malevolence that almost seemed directed at Hawk personally—caused a cold chill to run up his spine.

His eyes narrowed in concentration as he halted his mount and lifted his Hawken out of its saddle sling. To a casual observer, one glancing up at Hawk in a dark place perhaps, it might have appeared that a bear unaccountably dressed in a wide-brimmed hat and loose-fitting buckskins had dropped upon the back of a horse and now prowled above it, aping a human being. For Hawk was a giant of a man, huge in the shoulders and narrow in the gut, with a thick crop of golden hair that hung down clear to his shoulders, a face cut from granite, its aspect softened by a pair of sky-blue eyes; eyes that never failed to draw a woman—any woman he wanted.

Now, peering through the timber at the ridge, his preternaturally sharp eyes caught a sudden movement. Sunlight shifting on a tawny shape. He raised the rifle quickly enough, but found himself staring at an empty patch of blue sky. He lowered the rifle, feeling a mite sheepish. Even if he had caught the son of a bitch in his sights at this distance he would only be wasting precious shot and powder.

The ears of his mount and two packhorses flickered nervously. The two horses could smell the cougar. Dropping the rifle back in its sling, Hawk patted his mount on the neck to gentle it, then urged it on up the slope toward his cabin, the menace of the big mountain cat's angry snarl clinging to him like the shards of a bad dream. When he reached his barn, he caught sight of Raven Eyes behind the cabin on the edge of the timber. Shading her eyes, she was peering up at the ridge, her father's old flintlock in her hand.

She too had heard the cat.

He called out to her as he dismounted. Whirling about, she waved excitedly and started to run across the field toward him. Hawk was returning after a month of trapping in a small stream he had found deep in the Rockies. It had not been a waste of time; so hidden away had the stream been that it had never been completely trapped out like so many this side of the divide, and as a result Hawk was coming back with fifty prime plews, in addition to a bearskin and a wolfskin.

He led the horses into the barn and had just finished lifting the plews off the two packhorses when Raven Eyes reached the barn. They embraced with much enthusiasm, after which she insisted it was her place to tend to the horses and, suiting action to words, shooed him from the barn. Perfectly willing to let her take this chore off his hands, he lugged the furs into the cabin.

He was sprawled contentedly in the big wooden rocker when Raven Eyes came in. His boots were off and a jug of moonshine sat on the floor beside him. The plews, along with the wolfskin and the bearskin, he had dropped on the floor by the fireplace. He looked up as Raven Eyes closed the door firmly behind her and watched her lean the long flintlock into the corner beside the fireplace. As she started toward him, he watched her closely, drinking in every movement, realizing once again just how lovely she was, her eyes gleaming like a shimmering pool in a pine wood, her olive skin smooth over her high cheekbones, her shock of thick black hair flowing like a shimmering patch of midnight past the firm, taut breasts that swelled under her buckskin dress.

He wanted her so bad, he could taste it.

"Husband, I have a thing to tell you."

"I'm listening."

"You hear that big devil cat when you ride up?"

Hawk nodded. "He didn't sound very friendly."

"That is so, husband. He is angry with Raven Eyes."

"Now, why would that be?"

"The night after you go away, this big cat come down from the timber. He prowl close to barn. He want my pony, maybe. I load my father's gun and shoot him. I hit him but now he come back. I think he remembered what I did. Now he calls to me. He wants to punish me. His medicine is very powerful, I think."

"You sure you hit him?"

She nodded, her brows knit in a worried frown. "Yes, I hit him. In the thigh, I am sure. He went down, but he move off before I can reload and finish him."

"He did sound a mite unhappy. Looks like the wound is festering."

"I think maybe already he is cripple—or he not come after my pony."

"Maybe so. But now he is back. Only this time it is not just the pony he wants. Is that what you think?"

Raven Eyes looked at him very soberly, her black almond-shaped eyes mirroring her concern. "I think he is one very dangerous cat. And it is all my fault. I should have kill him first time."

"Maybe I better go out there now and finish him off." He started to get out of his chair.

"Stay in your chair, husband," she cried, alarmed. "That evil old cat will wait." Then she smiled down at him, her dark eyes smoldering. "But maybe I cannot wait. Already it is too long a wait for this woman."

He smiled up at her. "It's been a long time for this child, too."

He swept her into his arms and carried her into the small bedroom and dumped her unceremoniously onto the bed. As her back sank deep into the straw mattress, she hurriedly untied her shiftlike dress and flung it away; reaching up with quick hands, she peeled down his buckskins, and then he was crouched over her, plunging into her moist entrance with a wondrous ease, feeling her tightening about him like a fist. With a deep, heavy sigh, she drew him still deeper into her.

He buried his face in the wild luxuriance of her hair, prowling over her like a great snake. Eagerly she clung to him, wrapping her long limbs about his thighs, lunging up at him with a furious, savage intensity, meeting him thrust for thrust. The sound of her rapid breathing, the guttural cries that exploded from deep within her with each hammering thrust drove him to a wilder urgency—and he became lost completely in his mindless rush to completion.

It was over too quickly—almost as soon as it had begun, like a summer storm, as brief and as shattering. He flung back off her, exhausted. She shifted herself up on her elbows and gazed fondly at him.

"Rest now," she told him softly as she reached over and brushed a lock of damp hair off his forehead. "Then I fill tub for your bath and we eat fine supper."

"Sounds good."

"Then we make love again, slower. Until morning comes."

He tried to smile back up at her, but he was too exhausted even for that. His eyelids rested on his eyes as heavy as anvils. All he could manage was a faint nod as she got up from the bed and left the room. The last thing he remembered before a drugged sleep overwhelmed him was the snarling cry of the cougar echoing in the pines high above the cabin.

The next morning, the sun's first rays tipping the treetops, Hawk moved silently through the timber near the crest of the ridge, his Hawken primed and ready. Earlier, before dawn, he had been awakened by the nervous, restless stamping of the horses in the barn, and when he went out to investigate, he found fresh tracks left by the cat, which had circled the barn at least twice.

Now Hawk was following the big cat's spoor up toward the ridge's crest. Reaching it, he followed the cat's fresh tracks down the other side to the bank of a narrow stream. Splashing through the shallow water to the far side, Hawk went down on one knee to study the tracks more closely in the soft ground. They sure as hell were big enough, he reminded himself while he studied each paw's imprint carefully. As he had noticed from the beginning, the left hind paw track was turned in slightly, the imprint's edges smudged. It was obvious that for this cat, this injured foot was more an impediment than a help. Just as Raven Eyes had said, this was an old, nearly crippled cat.

Hawk stood up and looked around. He didn't like the look of this. No longer able to bring down his usual small game, probably in constant pain, ugly and spoiling for a fight—and maybe just a little desperate, this was now one very dangerous animal.

Hawk let his gaze follow the cat's tracks into the juniper lining the bank. Behind the juniper Hawk glimpsed a game trail that led up the timbered slope beyond the bank. Hawk mounted the bank, pushed through the junipers, and started up the game trail. He had gone about two hundred yards higher and was still deep in the timber when he halted to take a breather and get his bearings. The timber was quiet. From this height, he could see where the stream a half a mile or so farther on filtered into a bog. Somewhere in it a woodpecker was tapping at a tree trunk, while high above him in the treetops a robin sang, its clear call echoing in the pines. The sun was now well above the trees. It was going to be a warm day, very warm—one of the few good ones left in September; and if he wanted to get those furs to Fort Hall, he reminded himself, he had better leave soon, tomorrow maybe.

And forget about this damn cat.

Before starting back down the trail, Hawk took one last look around . . . and found himself staring directly into the cat's eyes. The cougar was poised on a low branch about twenty yards away, clearly visible through a gap in the branches. Crouching there, his head lowered, his mouth partly open in a silent snarl of contempt, he seemed to be challenging Hawk. And then he was gone, so swiftly and silently that Hawk could almost believe that that single, momentary glance had been a trick of his imagination.

He charged through the timber to the branch on which the cat had been crouching. Faint claw marks were clearly visible, and after a quick examination of the ground, Hawk found the spot where the cat had landed when he left the branch; but he found no further tracks on the pine-needle carpet. It was as if the big son of a bitch had vanished into thin air.

Distinctly uneasy, Hawk glanced about him in all directions—at the slope above, even the branches over his head. Nothing. Which one of us is the hunter? Hawk asked himself grimly.

He moved swiftly back down the slope and splashed across the stream, trying not to give himself the impression he was in flight, but that was how he felt, nevertheless. He had the odd conviction that the only reason the cat had not attacked him was because he had chosen not to do so.

Not this time, at least.

"I am the daughter of a chief," Raven Eyes told him proudly. "I do not run from this cougar."

"It ain't running, Raven Eyes," Hawk protested. "I just want your company on the trip to the fort."

"No, husband. I stay here to make you fine winter coat from this wolfskin. That other one is too old now."

Hawk knew what was going on here. Another woman had made his hooded wolfskin coat and Raven Eyes was anxious to replace it with one made by her. She had no reason to be jealous of a dead woman, but for her it made no difference to her that Hawk's former woman was dead. All that mattered was that he now wore a wolfskin coat made for him by another woman—and this she could not accept. If Hawk was her man, then she should be the one to make his clothes. No one else, living or dead, had that right.

"Then you're staying here?"

"Yes, husband."

"Be careful, then. Keep out of that cat's way. Don't take any more potshots at him."

"And if he disturbs my pony?"

"Ignore him. Just keep the barn door shut."

"You think I am such a fool to leave it open?"

"Just warning you, is all. You saw his tracks. He circled the barn twice. He's a cripple, and wants meat. He might already have tasted stock and grown to like it." He grinned slyly at her. "Maybe he's tasted Indian, too."

"Enough, husband," she told him. "Do not worry about this woman. Already she has spent many weeks alone with only the wind and the chatter of the chipmunks for company. So go now to the fort and do not forget the sugar and the salt."

He nodded solemnly. "I won't forget the licorice sticks, either."

She smiled. "And the looking glass you promised."

Hawk's fifty plews brought plenty, enough brass Made Beaver tokens to buy out the store. But it was the castoreum that really increased Hawk's credit with old MacPherson. The demand for the pungent medicinal oils secreted by the beaver's scent glands had increased over the past ten months, and the fort's chief factor was delighted with Hawk's plentiful haul of beaver stones.

A day after his arrival, anxious to get back, Hawk had already loaded his purchases onto his two packhorses, and by noon had left the gates of the fort behind him. In addition to the looking glass he had promised Raven Eyes, he carried three brown jugs of prime HBC rye whiskey to help him make it through the winter. The whiskey was from the chief factor's own prime, undiluted stock.

"Mr. Hawk!"

Reining in, Hawk turned to see a woman riding through the gate after him. She rode well, he noted. And when she got closer, he recognized her. She was Minerva Cantrell. The night before, she had arrived at the fort as a member of a wagon train of settlers on their way to the Oregon Territory. Her long red hair, which in a shocking breach of modesty she insisted on wearing combed out, her rosy cheeks, and her sparkling green eyes had not gone unnoticed at the fort. Not by Hawk, certainly, nor by any other man in the fort. A Crow half-breed made no effort to conceal his interest in her and had aroused MacPherson to warn the half-breed to keep a proper distance from her.

Handling her mount expertly, riding astride, not sidesaddle, the young woman pulled to a halt beside Hawk. "You must help me, Mr. Hawk."

"Name's Jed. Jed Thompson."

"Oh, I'm sorry. That hunchback with the black beard referred to you as Hawk, and I—"

"You talking about Buffalo Jim?"

"Is that his name?"

"It's what the Indians call him. With that hump he resembles a buffalo—to them, anyway."

"I see." She moistened her lips nervously. "He told me much about you, Mr. Thompson. You're a mountain man, I understand. And you live with an Indian squaw—"

"She's not a squaw, ma'am."

"Oh . . . ?" The sharpness in his tone caused her face to pale.

"She's a Crow Indian woman. Her name's Raven Eyes."

"I meant no discourtesy, Mr. Thompson. And I think that's a lovely name."

"What do you want, ma'am. I'm losing daylight sitting here."

"It's my brother. James Cantrell. You must help me find him."

"What makes you think I'd know him?"

"I understand he's living all by himself out here in the wilderness—hunting wild animals and trapping beaver."

"You'll have to do better than that, ma'am. There's quite a few men out here doing that—and more'n a few Indians, too."

"He's a big man—as big as you. You must help me find him."

"Sorry, ma'am. I got a piece to go yet, and I'm sure anxious to get there. Good-bye now." Hawk nudged his horse into motion.

"Mr. Thompson! Please!"

Hawk kept on riding. He hated to do it. But he sensed this Cantrell woman was the kind that didn't take no for an answer—not easily, that is—and he simply had no time for her.

"Mr. Hawk!" This time her voice was sharp, angry.

He glanced back without reining in.

"Is she that beautiful?"

Hawk's craggy face broke into a smile then. "Yes, ma'am. She sure as hell is."

He turned back around in his saddle and kept going. He did not look back.

Riding through a patch of timber two days later, Hawk felt a nagging uneasiness. The spruce timberland was alive with the chatter of birds and he could hear clearly the soft, distant sighing of the wind high in the trees; all about him as he rode were the swift, scuttling sounds of small animals fleeing his approach. The sunlight pouring down through the trees stamped bright, trembling patches of light over the forest floor. Yet, as he neared the edge of the timber, a brooding sense of menace increased and would not abate.

When he broke from the timber, he peered up the long meadow at his cabin and saw what he had prayed he would not see. The cabin doorway was gaping open, the darkness of the cabin's interior staring out at him ominously, reminding him of a skull's empty eye socket. Fighting panic, he flung aside the reins leading his packhorses and kicked his mount to a hard gallop up the slope.

At any moment he expected to see Raven Eyes step into view, either from the barn or from the rear of the cabin. But, despite the pounding of his horse's hooves, she did not appear. Where in hell was she?

At the cabin, Hawk flung himself from his horse and plunged through the open doorway. One glance about the cabin told him what he knew: the cabin was empty. But Raven Eyes had not been gone long. A stew was boiling away in a black pot over the fireplace. On top of the table lay the nearly completed wolfskin parka and jacket Raven Eyes had been working on. The hood and sleeves were already attached, the buttonholes sewn. She was waiting only for the buttons Hawk was bringing back with him.

Stepping back outside, he called, "Raven Eyes!"

His call echoed forlornly about the timbered slopes. He was about to call out again when he noticed the barn door was also wide open. He started toward it. As he got closer, he heard a dim thrashing sound.

Darting into the barn, he saw the cruelly slashed neck and shoulders of Raven Eyes' pony. Where its right rear leg should have been there were only raw tendons and white, splintered bone fragments. Hanging from the pony's muzzle were long, dusty ropes of dried lather. The horse's great brown eyes stared fixedly at the stall's side as it raised its head and slammed it down repeatedly with the mindless, steady persistence of a metronome. It seemed as if the poor dumb beast were trying deliberately to dash out its brains and end its misery.

Hawk stared at the deep claw marks and saw where jagged hunks of flesh had been ripped from the pony's shoulders. Beneath the animal there was a slick, fly-covered pool of dried blood, and Hawk wondered how in hell the pony could still be alive. Aiming his Colt through the cloud of flies, Hawk sent a slug into the pony's brain. Its head slammed down; its torn, bloody torso shuddered once, then lay still.

Outside the barn, Hawk found the cougar's tracks. Driven by its hunger, the huge mountain cat had broken into the barn by snaking past a loose board under the side window. The pony's cries had brought Raven Eyes running, and she was after him now, he realized. She was up there somewhere in the timber, lugging her father's flintlock, determined to show Hawk what a credit she was to her father. And she was also angry as hell at what that devil cat had done to her favorite pony.

Nearly at the timber, Hawk pulled up to call her name again. He waited for the echo of his call to die, then kept on into the woods. He found her tracks at the edge of the clearing where the ground was soft and not carpeted with pine needles, but after that her tracks vanished. He kept going until he reached the ridge where he had come upon the cat before, pulled up, and called out again to Raven Eyes.

This time she responded.

Dimly. The call came from high above him, it seemed. He turned, his eyes searching. The call came again. A little louder this time. There was no doubt now. It was Raven Eyes!

Altering his direction slightly, he redoubled his pace and scrambled on up through the brush and the timber, the slick carpet of pine needles causing him to slip to his knees more than once. He reached a tiny clearing, out of breath, panting, aware that he was no longer sure from which direction the cry from Raven Eyes had come.

He sucked in deep lungfuls of air, calmed himself, and called out again. This time the answering cry came from his right. He burst through a patch of timber toward it and came out upon another clearing, one he had never explored before, this one fronting a steep escarpment, at the base of which sat an impressive pile of granite boulders that had peeled off the cliff face. Some were as big as houses.

"Hawk!"

The call came from across the clearing, dimly.

Hawk scanned the edge of the clearing, then lifted his gaze to the top of the escarpment. He did not see Raven Eyes.

"Where are you?" he called.

"Up here!"

This time, peering more closely in the direction from which the cry came, Hawk saw Raven Eyes' pale face peering at him from a ledge halfway up the pile of rocks. He ran across the clearing, and when he reached the foot of the boulders, he halted and, shading his eyes, looked up at her.

"Are you all right?"

"Never mind me. Watch out for the cat!"

"Where is he?"

"Down there . . . I think."

Hefting his loaded rifle, Hawk glanced quickly around him, then up at the rocks past Raven Eyes. Nothing.

"I don't see him," he called up to her. "Come on down!"

"I can't."

"You hurt?"

She hesitated a moment, then nodded.

"I'll be right up."

She pulled back out of sight and he began to climb swiftly up through the rocks, feeling at times like a dwarf trying to negotiate some giant's front steps. At last he hauled himself up onto the ledge where Raven Eyes was crouching, and dropped to her side.

As he saw the extent of her injuries, he felt an icy blade of fear. She had been ripped cruelly from her shoulder to her thigh, the flesh laid open as cleanly as if a barber had used a safety razor, and lay in a dark pool of her blood. A flap of her scalp hung from the back of her head. She was lying on her side, her knees drawn up to her chin, hugging herself to keep her slashed breasts intact. Lifting her head, she looked at him unhappily, tears causing her large black eyes to shimmer. Though obviously in great pain, she did not utter a single word of complaint.

"My God, Raven Eyes," he gasped. "What happened?"

"That devil cat," she whispered fiercely. "I chase him from the barn, but he wait in the timber and take me. Then he drag me up here with him. I think now all he wants is me—not my pony."

Though on the face of it, the idea was preposterous, her words sent a shudder through Hawk and he jumped up to glance quickly around. "Which way did the son of a bitch go?" he asked her.

"I think maybe in the rocks above me. Be careful. I think maybe he want you, too."

"I sure as hell want him!"

Hawk looked back down at Raven Eyes. The single most important thing was to get Raven Eyes away from here and, from the look of her wounds, perhaps back to her people until she healed. But he now had the same respect for this mountain cat as did Raven Eyes. Neither he nor Raven Eyes would be going anywhere, he realized, until this cat was taken care of.

From where he was standing, Hawk could see beyond the clearing to the spruce- and fir-covered mountain flanks that fell away from it. At his back the sheer rock was scarred with massive cracks and pocked with at least three caves he could see for sure. With that sheer rock face at his back, a huge sprawl of boulders piled at his base, the damned cougar had an almost perfect redoubt from which he could issue forth whenever he was hungry—or angry.

Hawk studied intently the clefts and every cave entrance visible, then peered closely around him at the massive, disordered pile of granite slabs and boulders piled all about him and Raven Eyes.

The damned cat could be anywhere.

He heard Raven Eyes gasp, whirled, and saw her looking up past him at the cat crouching on a rock shelf just above him. Dropping to one knee, Hawk swung up his rifle. The cougar was in midair when Hawk pulled the trigger. Off balance when he fired, the rifle's powerful recoil knocked him flat. The cat took the bullet in his right shoulder, slammed down onto Hawk, his claws digging into his neck and chest, the crushing force of his muscled body grinding Hawk into the ledge. He felt the cat's great weight on his chest and felt the sickening snap as one of his ribs gave way. Poised on Hawk, his right shoulder streaming from the bullet wound, the cat turned his head and looked deep into Hawk's eyes. Then he snarled, uttering a cry so filled with savage fury his roar seemed to fill the universe. Dazed, and pinned by the enormous weight of the brute, Hawk could only wait.

In sudden, fierce outrage Raven Eyes flung herself on the cat's back and began beating and flailing at him with such mindless, inchoate fury that the cat—more astonished perhaps than threatened— turned on her and with one terrible swipe caught her on the side of the head, the blow powerful enough to send her flying back against a boulder. Able now to draw his bowie, Hawk plunged it repeatedly into the cat's exposed flank, each thrust driving the blade in almost clear to the hilt. With a startled, infuriated screech, the cat swiped at Hawk, the claws narrowly missing his face, then sprang up onto a rock and vanished from sight.

Dimly aware that he was bleeding steadily from his neck and that at least one of his ribs had caved in, all Hawk could think of was Raven Eyes. He crawled to her side and saw that she was no longer conscious.

He bent his head to her chest. Her heart was thudding—faintly, but steadily. Sheathing the bowie, Hawk tossed his rifle to the clearing below, flung Raven Eyes over his back, and carried her down from the rocks, ignoring the excruciating pain that erupted in his chest each time he reached out for a handhold. He was at a great distance from himself, watching his climb down through the rocks with icy detachment.

When he reached the clearing, he picked up his rifle and continued into the timber with Raven Eyes still slung over his back, not returning back into himself, it seemed, until he reached the cabin, had bathed and bound her torn body, and soothed her into a restful sleep at last.

Then—and only then—did he allow himself to drop, barely conscious, onto the bed beside her.

—2—

Buffalo Jim placed the mug of rum onto the plank table in front of Hawk, then slumped down across from him and drew his own rum closer. A glimpse of Hawk brooding in a corner of Fort Hall's grog shop without a drink in front of him had prompted Big Jim to purchase a mug of rum for Hawk and invite himself over to his table.

Jim was a heavily bearded, shambling hulk of a man with a hump on his back near as big as a buffalo's—and most of the time the wide, trusting eyes of a child. The hump caused him to stoop some, but not much; and to the credulous Indians hereabouts, he was Buffalo Man, a mighty personage with great and terrible powers, a conviction Big Jim used to his considerable advantage when dealing with them.

Now, leaning closer over the table, he seemed genuinely concerned about Hawk. "Drink that down, hoss," he urged kindly. "It'll give you a boost right into next week."

Hawk lifted the mug to his lips and threw a good portion of its contents down his throat. The fiery liquor scorched a trail clear to his stomach, then sent its warm tentacles out to his fingertips and clear down to his toes. He nodded grimly at Big Jim. "Much obliged, Jim."

"Ain't nothin' wrong in this godforsaken wilderness don't seem to sit better with the stomach on fire and the head spinnin'."

"I reckon so, Jim."

"'Course, you bein' half Injun, I guess it wouldn't do for you to drink too much of that."

Hawk snapped his head up to look at the big mountain man and discovered him smiling, his wide blue eyes as innocent of malice as a child's.

"Thought that'd get a rise out of you," Buffalo Jim said, chuckling. He lifted his mug and gulped down what rum remained in it, then wiped off his mouth with the back of his hairy paw. His thick, silken beard covered his face almost completely, and he kept it as clean as a grizzly's muff. "You want to talk about it, hoss? I kin see you got the miseries. I heard tell your woman's gone back to her people."

"That's where she is, all right."

"Why, hell, Hawk. Don't give it no never mind. Women is like the wind. Sometimes warm, sometimes chill, and always movin'."

"She was hurt, Jim. Hurt bad. I'm hoping her people can pull her through."

"By God, Hawk, I didn't know that. Had no idea. What be the trouble?"

Hawk told Jim about the cougar. When he finished, the big man leaned back with a frown on his face and shook his head in wonderment.

"Hell's fire, hoss, you're lucky to be here your own self."

Hawk shrugged and took a sip of the rum. Jim

was right, of course. He was lucky to be alive. And if it hadn't been for Raven Eyes, there was a good chance that he would not be here now, telling his story to Buffalo Jim. While most of the lacerations in his neck had pretty well healed by now, his cracked ribs still gave him trouble; every time he took a deep breath he could feel them protesting.

"Just how bad *is* Raven Eyes?" Jim asked, his blue eyes showing genuine concern.

"When I left her, she was out of her head with fever. Didn't recognize me. Kept seeing that damn cat prowlin' inside her father's lodge. Said he was maulin' her. Said she could feel his hot breath on her." Hawk shook his head grimly, his granitic, hawklike face set with an iron resolve. "I'm goin' after that cat, Jim. I'm going to track that old bastard clear to hell if that's what it takes."

"I'll be glad to sign on with you for the duration, Hawk—if you'll have me."

"Thanks, Jim. I appreciate that. But I want to finish that son of a bitch myself."

"I guess I can understand that."

"Now, let me fill up these mugs."

"I'd take that kindly, Hawk. I surely would."

As Hawk was returning to the table, Chief Factor MacPherson intercepted him. "Heard you were in here, Hawk. I'd like a word with you—soon as you can manage it."

"What's wrong with right now? Join Jim and me here at the table."

"If you don't mind, Hawk."

As soon as MacPherson had settled into a chair, he told Hawk he had heard about Raven Eyes and sympathized, but right at the moment he needed help to get out of a queer, unsettling quandary, and he hoped that Hawk might see his way clear to helping him.

"No need for all that preamble, Mac," Hawk told the man. "Out with it. What's your problem?"

"It's a woman. Minerva Cantrell. Same one as accosted you when you were leaving the fort last time."

"The one looking for her brother? You mean she's still here?"

"Yes, she sure as hell is, Hawk."

"And she still wants someone to help her find her brother?"

MacPherson nodded unhappily.

"I'm not going looking for him, Mac. I got problems of my own. I just came back for provisions and more lead and gunpowder."

"Just hear me out, Hawk."

Hawk took his mug and leaned back in his chair. "All right, Mac. I'll hear you out. But that doesn't mean I'm going to be listening very hard."

"The thing is, Hawk, her brother's not lost anymore. I know where he is, and so does she. Only now she wants to go out after him—alone!"

Hawk frowned. "Maybe you better explain."

"He's with Spotted Pony, the Blackfoot chief."

"What the hell's he doing with him?" Jim broke in. "That's one mean Blackfoot. And them bastards don't allow no white trappers in there. Not unless they get a fresh scalp in exchange."

"He's right, Mac," Hawk pointed out. "You sure this trapper is still alive?"

"He's alive, all right. Fact is, this Cantrell feller is not any trapper I ever heard of—fact is, he's got some crazy idea he'd like to civilize these savages and start his own kingdom. Of course, he must be as mad as a hatter, but the Blackfoot are treatin' him with considerable awe and appreciation. He's teachin' them how to fight—the white man's way, that is."

"So tell the woman to leave her brother be," Buffalo Jim said, grinning. "He's doin' just fine, looks like."

"I wish it were as simple as that, Jim. The thing is, her brother has convinced Spotted Pony that his medicine will enable him to wipe out all their enemies."

"Is this Cantrell in any danger?"

"I don't think so. Not now, anyway. 'Course, you never can trust a Blackfoot."

"Well, then, there's nothing anyone can do for him, Mac," Hawk said. "Sure he's crazy, and so is Spotted Pony for believing him, but we can't be responsible for every nut who leaves this fort."

"Then do an old man a favor, Hawk. Go tell his sister this before she pulls out. Speak to her. See if you can talk some sense into her. If she gets away from this here fort and vanishes into them mountains, I'll never hear the end of it."

"Hell, Mac. Just don't let her go."

"How can I stop her? You want me to arrest her? Lock her up? And I sure as hell can't shoot her, Hawk. She's free, white, and over twenty-one."

Hawk glanced over to Buffalo Jim. The huge mountain man shrugged. "Won't do any harm to talk to her, will it, Hawk?"

Hawk looked at MacPherson. "All right, then. I'll talk to her."

"I sure do appreciate it, Hawk."

"But that's all I'll do: *talk* to her. If she won't listen to reason, then we'll just have to let her do what she thinks is best—no matter what."

"Just speak to her, Hawk."

Hawk finished his rum, got to his feet, and followed MacPherson from the grog shop.

They found Minerva Cantrell in front of the stables, getting ready to move out. She had purchased two packhorses, which were now heavily laden with camping equipment, a tent, provisions, and other essentials. Money, it seemed, was no object. If she was the one who had loaded and packed the horses, Hawk had to admit she knew what she was doing.

She was dressed sensibly as well, wearing thick, woolen pants, heavy leather high-top shoes, a man's heavy cotton shirt, and over that a sheepskin jacket. Atop her flaming red hair she had set a black felt, floppy-brimmed hat. Dressed entirely in men's attire though she was, there was no doubt in Hawk's mind that this was a strikingly beautiful—and very determined—young lady.

At their approach, she thrust out her sharp, bold chin, and with an icy glare at Hawk she let him know she not only recognized him, but recalled his refusal to help her.

"Miss Cantrell," MacPherson began, "this here's Jed Thompson."

"Is that his name—really?"

"Some call him Golden Hawk," MacPherson admitted.

"Do they, now?"

"Miss Cantrell," Hawk spoke up, "I came out here at the chief factor's request. I assure you, I have no desire to stop you from doing whatever it is you want to do."

"Fine. Then I hope both of you will get out of my way." She glanced coldly at Hawk. "I'm losing daylight." She turned then to step into her stirrup.

Hawk strode quickly forward and helped her up into the saddle. "There's just one thing, Miss Cantrell."

"And what might that be, Mr. Thompson?" she asked, gathering up her reins.

"Do you think you're going to do your brother any good without your scalp or tied up to some buck's lodgepole with a piece of rawhide?"

Hawk saw her face lose its color. But she met his gaze without flinching. "I'll have you know, Mr. Thompson, that my brother is the guest of Chief Spotted Pony. All I intend to do is join him and do what I can to convince him to return with me to civilization."

"Just a walk in the park, huh?"

She reached for the reins to her packhorses. Hawk obligingly handed them to her. "I suppose you've told your brother you're on the way so he can alert the Blackfoot bands to keep an eye out for you—see that you don't get lost, that sort of thing."

"He has no idea I have come this far. Don't be silly."

Hawk stepped back and met her gaze without flinching. "Miss Cantrell, aren't you the one being silly?"

"I don't know what you mean," she snapped icily.

"What he means, Miss Cantrell," broke in Mac-

Pherson, stepping closer, "is it's a long way from here to Blackfoot Territory. Through pretty wild country, filled with savages who have no treaty with the white man and no great liking for him, either."

"You can go it alone if you've a mind to," Hawk finished off, "but you are sure as hell making it tough on Mr. MacPherson here. He'll consider himself responsible for what happens."

Minerva Cantrell, eyes flashing, looked from one to the other, as if they were recalcitrant schoolchildren who were refusing to learn their alphabet. "Don't you see? Either of you? This is my brother. I must go after him. I have no choice."

Hawk stepped away from her horse. "Then suit yourself, Miss Cantrell. And good luck to you."

"Our prayers go with you," said MacPherson regretfully.

"Thank you, gentlemen," she said. She wheeled her horse and rode out, leading her packhorses at a brisk pace.

The two men stood where they were and watched her approach, then pass through the gate. Hawk swore softly.

"Damn," he said to Mackenzie. "I hoped she was bluffing."

"Not that one. No sir."

"The way she sees it, she's got no choice."

"She must be real close to that fool brother of hers."

Hawk turned and started for the other end of the stables.

"Where you goin', Hawk."

Hawk paused. "To see to my horse. Then I

guess I'll be picking up my possibles and some fresh jerky."

"You mean you ain't stayin' on tonight?"

For answer, Hawk simply glanced after Miss Minerva Cantrell riding across the meadow beyond the gate.

MacPherson smiled in sudden relief. "Pick up what you need from my chief clerk, Hawk. Anything. Anything at all. No charge."

"That's real decent of you, Mac."

"Just bring her back in one piece."

Hawk promised nothing as he continued on into the stables. He wasn't going to make any promises he couldn't keep. With this headstrong redhead, a man was a damn fool to make any.

Hawk overtook Minerva Cantrell at dusk, approaching her camp from a ridge above it.

For most of the afternoon, Hawk had followed the woman without making any effort to overtake her, content to scout ahead and along her route to keep a lookout for any hostiles in the area. He had sighted a Crow hunting party, but they apparently had no idea Minerva Cantrell was moving through their land, and as soon as Hawk had determined there was no likelihood the hunting party would cross Minerva's path, he was content to stay out of sight until the Crows had proceeded on their way.

When he moved across the small clearing flanking Minerva Cantrell's camp, he noted that she had chosen her site well. Except for the willow clumps lining the small stream on the bank of which she had pitched her tent, there was no way a raiding party could approach her camp without crossing an open space that afforded little or no cover.

He rode straight across the clearing until he came to the stream, then moved up it, moving out into its shallows when he neared the willows. Breaking through them, he rode up onto the bank, expecting to find the Cantrell woman in front of her tent. She was not there. He reined up, startled, and looked quickly around. No sign of her. Damn. Some scatterbrain, he figured. More than likely off wandering about without a weapon looking for mushrooms or some such nonsense.

He heard a slight sound to his right, turned, and saw Minerva Cantrell step out of the willows, a rifle in her hand, its muzzle yawning up at him. She held it steadily, unwavering, a slight, grim smile on her face as she advanced.

"Are you going to explain what you're doing here, Mr. Thompson?"

"Isn't that obvious?"

"No, it isn't. I thought I left you back at Fort Hall."

"I wish you had."

Minerva lowered the rifle. "Light, Mr. Thompson. I was preparing coffee when you approached. If you'll be patient, I'll make a fresh pot."

"I'd appreciate it."

Hawk dismounted and led his horse closer to the stream, offsaddled it, rubbed the animal down, then hobbled it and returned to the campfire. The coffee was ready. Minerva handed him a steaming cup. He took it from her and sipped it.

"I have some jerky," he told her. "Over there by my saddle."

"And so do I, Mr. Thompson. It seems I am as well-prepared as you are . . . and just as careful."

"I noticed."

"Perhaps I should tell you. I have ridden quite extensively throughout the Adirondack Mountains back East, and camping out is something my brother and I have been doing since we were children. So you see, Mr. Thompson, when it comes to the wilderness, I am not such an innocent as you might think."

"They have Blackfoot tribes in the Adirondacks, do they?"

"No, they don't. And there are no grizzlies, either. Yes, Mr. Thompson, I am quite aware of the dangers to be found in this wilderness. Mr. MacPherson and everyone else I have talked to since coming out here have made that abundantly clear. But it happens that I am an excellent shot."

"That's just fine. I'm glad. Does this mean you want me to return to Fort Hall?"

She laughed. "Of course not. In fact, I'm glad you're here. With you at my side, I feel much better about the possibility of reaching my brother safely. Now just make yourself comfortable while I rustle up something to eat. I don't know about you, but I'm famished."

"Just one thing."

"And what's that?"

"Call me Jed."

"And you can call me Alice."

"Alice?"

"It's my middle name. I prefer it to Minerva."

"Alice it is, then."

Alice did wonders with the jerky and beans,

frying the jerky to a crisp tenderness close to bacon and cooking the beans in brown sugar. Her coffee, sweetened with honey, was just right. Sitting by her fire while she cooked their meal, Hawk felt a little foolish. Maybe this woman had no need of him, after all. Him or any other man. She was that self-sufficient, it seemed.

He had settled into his sugan for the night farther downstream close to the horses when he heard, then saw, her making her way toward him through the darkness. He sat up as she crouched beside him. In the bright moonlight he saw she was wearing only a pale nightdress and slippers and had combed her red hair out so that it fell in one shimmering blade onto her lap. She placed a small silken pillow on the ground beside him and made herself comfortable on it.

"You'll get a chill coming out here like that," he told her.

"Perhaps."

He knew she expected him to lift his blanket and invite her in under it, but he had no intention of doing so. He liked her well enough, but he hardly knew her and he didn't want to get things too complicated this soon, and it sure as hell would make matters a mite thicker. Besides, he knew he would only be thinking of Raven Eyes when he did. And that wouldn't be fair to her.

She hugged her knees and glanced past him at the stream, then began to hum softly. It was a pleasant-enough tune and Hawk thought he might have heard it somewhere before—far in the past. It might have been a ballad his parents had sung as they rolled westward over the Texan landscape.

"What's that you're humming?"

"A Shaker tune: 'It's Good to Be Simple.' "

"I like it."

"The Shakers don't believe in relations between the sexes . . . not carnal, I mean."

"So they sing that song instead?"

She laughed lightly, softly, and turned her green eyes on him. In the darkness they appeared to glow. "Yes."

"Not such a bad idea, I suppose. Keeps you out of trouble."

"I suppose. If you *want* to keep out of trouble."

"Which you don't."

"What do you think, Mr. Golden Hawk?"

"Call me Jed."

"I prefer your real name, Hawk. I like it. Do you know, your face has the same fierce, haughty look about it as a hawk—or an eagle, especially that sharp beak of a nose. And those clear blue eyes of yours seem capable of looking so far, so deep . . . maybe right into a person's soul. And right now perhaps you don't particularly like what you find in mine."

He thought maybe he knew what she was getting at, but he was determined she would not have her way. Once this filly got the bit in her teeth, she would be off to the races and it would take one hell of a rider to hang on.

She sensed his pulling back and looked at him for a long moment before she said, "That woman of yours—Raven Eyes—do you think she will be jealous when she hears of you escorting me through this wilderness?"

He took a deep breath. Talk of Raven Eyes at this moment brought actual, physical pain. "She is with her people," he told her, his voice tight.

Alice's eyebrows went up a notch. "You mean she's abandoned you, gone back to her aboriginal relations?"

"No. She's close to death. She was mauled by a cougar. There was nothing I could do for her, so her people are taking care of her. At the moment I'm not sure she's still alive. If you don't mind, I'd rather not talk any more about her."

Abashed, her voice low and filled with concern, she said, "I'm . . . sorry. Terribly sorry. I didn't know."

"Forget it," he told her, eager to change the subject. "And while I think of it, let me ask something I've been wondering about for a while now. How come Mac and you know so much about your brother and his whereabouts?"

"Three days ago a Nez Percé Indian and his squaw came to the fort to trade. The woman was educated by a missionary and spoke English. It seems my brother is creating quite a stir among the Blackfoot tribes. It was Mr. MacPherson who heard about James first and then brought the two Nez Percé Indians to me so I could question them."

"You're sure it's your brother with Spotted Pony?"

"Yes. The Nez Percé woman's description of him matched perfectly."

"I'm surprised. A man changes a lot once he gets out here."

"You mean he sheds a lot, he becomes . . . someone else."

"Maybe he becomes what he really is—not what that eastern civilization tries to tell him he is."

"You don't like the East, do you?"

"No, I don't."

"But how could you possibly judge the East or anyone from it? All you know is this wild, savage land—and the savages who live here. You see, Mr. Golden Hawk, I've heard all about you. You're part Comanche, part white man. You were brought up by the Comanches. There's white blood in you, of course. Your long, blond hair and blue eyes attest to that. But you're more Comanche than white man. Your soul is that of a true savage. I can sense it."

She was almost out of breath when she finished, having spoken in a sudden rush. It was clear she had been waiting a long time to get that off her chest.

"You finished now?"

She nodded—somewhat ruefully, he thought.

"That was a long speech, Alice."

She tried not to notice the cold anger in his eyes. "Yes, I guess it was. I really didn't mean to go on like that. I suppose I put my foot in my mouth again."

"There's a sure way to prevent that."

"Oh . . ."

"That's right. Just learn to keep your mouth shut."

Her pale cheeks flamed. "You *are* a savage. A perfect savage!"

"Good night, Minerva."

He thought she was going to strike him. She didn't. He lay calmly back down and pulled his sugan's blanket up over his shoulders and turned his back on her, grinning broadly, waiting for her anger to explode. Instead, she got quickly to her feet and marched back to her tent.

He breathed a sigh of relief and closed his eyes.

Late the next afternoon, Hawk pulled his horse up and waited for Alice to reach him.

"We got company—and soon," he told her.

"What do you mean?"

He smiled thinly. "What you call aborigines, savages."

"But I've seen no sign of anyone."

"You haven't been looking very hard, then. Notice how quiet the woods are? And those crows that took flight a few minutes back—off to our right? And then there's something else. Never fails me."

"What's that?"

"The hair on the back of my neck. It sort of springs to attention when I'm being watched."

"That's silly. You've been reading too many books."

"The thing is, I don't want you to panic when they show up. Just watch me. And listen. Now prime and load that rifle of yours and let it rest across your pommel. Just in case."

"You *are* serious!"

"Ma'am, will you stop prattling and do as you're told!"

She was about to make a retort, but thought better of it. As she reached for her rifle, he spurred on ahead of her.

For the next half-hour or so, they rode on steadily, with no sign of trouble, but the hair on the back of Hawk's neck did not relax any and his horse became increasingly skittish. He attempted to peer through the gloom that filled the timber on all sides of them, but saw only shadows of shadows. Alice rode along behind him calmly enough, her loaded rifle resting across the pommel of her saddle as he had instructed, but before long he caught in her gaze something akin to scorn at his caution and obvious nervousness. She apparently thought he was close to falling apart, so much like an old woman had he become, and all because he had seen a few crows take wing.

Hawk was nearly across a small clearing when the first Bannock broke from the timber in front of him and pulled up, his face somber. He wore no war paint, but none was needed for these mischievous pirates of the forest. Of Shoshone stock, they exhibited little of the fine qualities so much in evidence among the true Shoshoni—honor and courage, for starters. They were content to smile their way into a white man's confidence, then stab him in the back on the first opportunity. Hawk realized how difficult it was going to be to deal with them at that moment, especially with Alice Cantrell in tow. He would almost have preferred dealing with Blackfoot than with these unprincipled bastards.

Hawk was not surprised when two other Bannocks appeared on his flanks. Glancing behind him, he saw a fourth Indian breaking from the timber behind Alice. She was holding up fine, he saw, her expression calm. He reined in until she was abreast of him.

"They don't look so dangerous," she whispered to him nervously.

"Just give them time . . . and an opportunity."

Suddenly the four Bannocks let loose with a

series of shattering war cries and lashed their horses to a gallop, coming directly at Hawk and Alice. Within twenty or so yards, they turned their mounts and galloped around them, drawing the circle tighter with each pass.

Hawk sat his horse quietly, waiting for the game to end, while beside him Alice clutched her rifle, her face grim.

The show ended as swiftly as it had begun with the Bannocks slamming into them and flinging them off their horses, then leaping from their ponies' backs to finish them off. Hawk landed hard, the ground slamming into his back with such force that he found himself gasping for breath. He heard Alice scream and, glancing over, saw her still on her feet, wrestling furiously with one of the Bannocks who was trying to take her rifle.

With a sudden, impatient grunt, the Bannock kicked Alice in the crotch. She let go of the rifle and went flying back. Turning the rifle on Hawk then, the Bannock was about to fire down at him when Hawk rolled over, drew his Colt, and fired up at the Bannock. The bullet caught the Indian in the face, destroying it. Hawk kept on rolling and blasted another Bannock in the gut with his second round, sprang to his feet, and took careful aim on a third Bannock. Before he could fire, a Bannock war club caught him from behind.

He heard Alice's scream as he spun to the ground and momentarily lost consciousness. When he regained his senses he saw the two remaining Bannocks standing over him. One of them was holding Alice by her hair, clutching it so tightly that tears of pain and outrage boiled out of her eyes. Determined not to give either of these Bannocks the satisfaction of seeing her cry out, she uttered not a sound.

The Bannock who had clubbed Hawk stepped forward and kicked Hawk's Colt out of his hand, then hauled him upright and lifted his bowie from its sheath. Then he smiled and kicked Hawk in the groin. When Hawk jackknifed forward, the Bannock brought up his knee, smashing Hawk just under his nose. Hawk felt his lips blossom under the impact. It felt as if his nose had been broken as well. But he said nothing as he sagged to one knee, then reached up to feel his chin. It was sticky and warm with his blood.

Abruptly, his hand swept past his chin and he twisted away from the Bannock, reaching back behind his heavy nap of hair for his throwing knife as he ran. The Bannock raced after him, apparently thinking Hawk was only desperate to escape further punishment. Hawk pulled up sharply, whirled, and before the surprised Bannock could protect himself, thrust the knife into the Indian's gut. The blade sank deep and Hawk clung to it resolutely, tugging it upward, past the belly button. When he withdrew the blade, black blood followed out after it and poured like a spring freshet over his wrist.

He ducked back quickly out of the way. The Bannock, astonished, stared down at the gushing hole in his belly. He grabbed at it in an effort to stem the flow and tried to cry out, but he had no voice. His knees gave way and he collapsed forward onto his spilled guts.

The other Bannock had already flung Alice

aside and was raising his own flintlock pistol. At that range, Hawk realized, he could blow a hole in Hawk as big as a fist. Alice must have realized the same thing. With a cry she rushed at the Bannock, destroying his aim a split second before the pistol detonated. The lead ball plowed into the ground at Hawk's feet.

The Bannock snatched Hawk's Walker Colt off the ground. Alice tried to wrest it from him, but he cracked her head with it, then cocked the weapon and leveled it at Hawk. About to rush the Bannock, Hawk pulled up. The distance between them was too great. Hawk saw the Bannock's finger tighten on the trigger and was about to throw himself to his left when the crack of a rifle echoed across the clearing. The Bannock's right side exploded. He sagged down onto one knee and looked up at Hawk in pure astonishment as Hawk reached him in four quick strides and wrested the huge Walker Colt from his grasp and smashed the Bannock on the top of the head with it. As the Indian keeled forward onto the grass, Hawk heard the soft drum of hooves and looking up, saw Buffalo Jim, a Kentucky rifle resting across his pommel, gallop out of the timber toward them.

Hawk had never been so glad to see anyone in his life. He waved. Jim waved back.

"My God," said Alice, getting slowly to her feet. "Who's that?"

"Buffalo Jim. The man who just saved our guts."

Weasel Piss, a Kwahadi Comanche of twenty years with only one disputed coup to his credit and not a single scalp, stepped back into the timber, cursing his gods at Golden Hawk's luck.

Tall and powerfully built, unusually lanky for a Comanche, with black, intelligent eyes, Weasel Piss had not been a party to the ill-fated Bannock attack on Golden Hawk and the woman. No Comanche would ever allow himself to become an ally of the stinking Bannocks, the root-eaters of the northern mountains. They were a people without pride or conquest, miserable blanket Indians of the timbered foothills, though they rode fine horses on occasion and now and then pitched their lodges on the high plains and ate buffalo meat like their betters.

Weasel Piss had planned to wait until the Bannocks captured Golden Hawk and then steal upon the Bannock camp and take the hated ex-Comanche slave from them—perhaps at the same time removing a few Bannock scalps. Now Weasel Piss would have to bide his time and take Golden Hawk with no aid from the Bannocks. This was not a pleasant prospect, especially when he took the measure of the hunchbacked mountain man now dismounting beside Golden Hawk and the woman.

The young Comanche warrior melted back into the timber and hurried up the slope to his waiting pony.

The stubby paint was a present from Coyote Heart, his only rival for the maiden Willow Tree's affection. That the pony had little endurance and was chronically sore-footed deeply troubled Weasel Piss, for he realized that Coyote Heart had deliberately presented him with a mount of questionable stamina. But this betrayal by a comrade he had thought was his friend only steeled Weasel Piss's resolve. He would let nothing stop him from taking Golden Hawk.

In this way would he shame Coyote Heart for his betrayal ... and win the daughter of a chief.

—3—

As Buffalo Jim dismounted, he doffed his floppy hat to Alice, then looked over at Hawk. "You two look a mite shook up," he said. "But I can't say as I blame you none."

"Where the hell did you come from?" demanded Hawk.

"Why, hoss, that's clear enough, ain't it? From them woods back there."

"You been following us?"

"Yep. Got it into my head maybe you two could use another hand. This here's wild country."

"Yes," said Alice. She ran her fingers nervously through her disheveled red hair, then bent to pick up her hat. "I am beginning to realize that. This certainly is wild country. I am most grateful you caught up to us when you did."

"Yeah, thanks, Jim," Hawk said.

"Hoss, we better get a move on. These here hills is filled with Bannocks—most of them as mad as wet hornets."

"How come?"

"They just got their asses whupped by a Blackfoot war party led by Spotted Pony."

Alice came alert. "Did you say Spotted Pony?"

"That's who I said, sure enough."

Alice turned to Hawk, her eyes bright with excitement. "Why, Jed! That's the chief my brother's with. That means he's close by."

"Sorry to disappoint you, ma'am," Jim told her. "That Blackfoot war party's long gone. Been gone for close onto a week. From all accounts, Spotted Pony's campin' quite a bit north of here, near the Powder River."

"Which means we better get a move on," Hawk reminded her. "Like Jim just told us. Before these here Bannocks we just messed up are missed."

In a few moments they were on their way, riding on into the timber. Hawk saw Alice glance back once at the bodies strewn on the grass behind them. She turned about resolutely and continued on into the timber without a word.

They made a dry camp without a fire on a low, pine-covered bluff. It was clear Alice would have preferred water and fire to cook with, but after her encounter with those Bannocks, she went along without a murmur and soon rolled into her blanket and closed her eyes.

She was still shaken by that Bannock attack, Hawk realized. It was not the night's chill alone that was causing her to shiver every now and then, but an understandable reaction—even if delayed—to that sudden, unprovoked attack. She had been cruelly used, kicked, and knocked brutally to the ground, then hauled upright by her hair. She was lucky to have escaped with her life. That she had taken it with so little complaint impressed Hawk.

"Guess I'll sleep down there," Jim said, indicating the base of the bluff. "Any more of them beggars try to take us, they'll have to get past me."

Hawk nodded and watched Buffalo Jim pick his way down the slope, moving silently and swiftly, despite his great bulk. He was soon out of sight in the darkening clump of scrub juniper growing at the base of the bluff.

"Will he be all right?" Alice asked, sitting up suddenly to peer down the slope.

"Buffalo Jim's a tough man to hurt—or surprise."

"I suppose. It's too bad."

"What's too bad?"

"His back. That . . . awful hump."

"Ma'am," Hawk said, his voice icy with anger, "I don't know what the hell you're talking about. I don't see no hump—none at all."

His tone caused her to flinch, and at once he regretted his anger, but he didn't see how he could have helped himself. Her tone of pity, combined with an unmistakable tinge of disgust, had angered him deeply. Buffalo Jim was no man to pity, and despite his rough exterior, he was a gentleman from sole to crown.

Though she tried to hold her tears back, Alice suddenly bent her head and began sobbing quietly. At once Hawk was beside her, his arms about her shoulders, his murmured apology getting nowhere against the storm of tears now bursting from her. But he kept his arms about her and gradually her crying subsided.

"I'm all right," she said eventually. "I don't know why I'm so touchy all of a sudden."

"Forget it. You've been through a hell of a lot today."

Still in his arms, she dug at her eyes with her fists and told him miserably, "I don't blame you for being angry with me. You're right. Jim's a fine man—and very brave."

"No need for you to apologize. It's all forgotten now." He released her.

"No," she whispered, reaching out for him. "Please. Don't take your arms away. Not now."

Hawk pulled her close again. Since the moment he had ridden away from Raven Eyes' village—not knowing for sure if he would ever see her alive again—a chill had fallen over his soul, a chill and a terrible emptiness. Now, with Alice Cantrell's cheek against his chest, her arms hugging him tightly, he felt the emptiness inside him begin to fill.

Reaching back, Alice lifted her blanket and without a word he slid in under it beside her. For a long while they let the warm closeness of each other soothe them. At last she spoke up, softly.

"That business with the Bannocks. I can't get it out of my mind."

"Try."

"That's not easy. Now, for the first time, I realize something I hadn't grasped before."

"What's that?"

"That there's a chance we might die in this godforsaken wilderness. That I might never find James."

"I guess there's always that possibility."

She lifted her face to his. "In that case, there's something I want first."

Hawk pulled her closer and smiled at her. "I think maybe that's something we both want."

With lightning-swift fingers she unbuttoned the front of her nightgown while he peeled off his buckskin pants. Eagerly, she pressed her naked body hard against his. It fit like a silken sheath. He took one of her breasts in his hand and kissed her on the lips, on the neck, under her ear. She moaned softly as he nibbled on one of her earlobes.

The warmth of her was melting him; it was as if he had opened the door to a thundering wood stove. His lips explored the incandescence of her firm breasts, then moved down her belly, his rough fingers flicking her rigid nipples. She began to moan softly.

He took her lips in his. They softened, opened eagerly for his probing tongue, the sweet scent of her arousal inflaming him. Her hands had already found his erection. Feverishly, she stroked it. He had been without a woman for too long, he realized, and would not be able to play with her much longer.

He grabbed her hips and shoved her under him. She spread her thighs to make it easier for him to enter. He thrust eagerly forward, flowing effortlessly into her warmth. Sighing, she sucked him in still deeper, then began undulating with measured, sinuous movements while Hawk probed still deeper into her, content for the moment to feel her inner muscles squeezing him like a fist.

Abruptly, she came, shuddering gently. He let her have her way, waiting patiently, pleased he had succeeded so well in arousing her. And then her happy convulsions were done. She relaxed and lay motionless under him, her arms still tight about his neck. He too was on the verge of exploding, his erection still solid, still pulsing deep within her. She began to move again, rotating her hips slowly, deliberately. He pushed himself forward and plunged deeper into her. She gasped and, flinging up her legs, dug both heels into his back, lifting her hips off the ground as she did so. With a happy grunt, he lunged still deeper into her, striking bottom each time—and then, to his astonishment, he felt her quake as another climax shook her. This one lasted longer than the first, and when it was done, she smiled mischievously up at him and sighed in absolute contentment, a deep flush suffusing her face.

"Don't hold back any longer," she whispered eagerly.

Needing no further urging, he lunged deep into her, exalting in her sharp, eager cry of pleasure as he struck bottom. Again and again he fathomed her hot depths. There was no holding back now. He couldn't, even if he had wanted to.

"Yes! Yes, Hawk," she panted.

He grinned down at her. "Is this what you want?"

"I want every inch! Don't hold back!"

Arching above her, he slammed still deeper, the flood building in him until he felt himself sweeping over the edge, dimly aware of her tossing head, of her fingers digging into his back. At last the dam burst. He felt himself being sucked clean, his ejaculation so powerful and prolonged it was almost painful. As she felt him pulsing uncontrollably inside her, she hugged him even more tightly, uttering tiny cries that became at last a long, sobbing moan . . . and then silence.

Hawk relaxed, still on top of her, too spent to move. She bore his weight without murmur, her arms wrapped happily about him, staring up into his eyes, her own gleaming with the pleasure he had just given her.

"I'm not finished," he told her.

"I know," she said, pulling his face down onto her breasts and caressing his thick blond hair. "I can still feel you."

Then, laughing softly, she pushed Hawk over onto his back and mounted him swiftly.

He grinned up at her as she impaled herself eagerly upon his shaft and leaned back. A deep sigh escaped her. With a quick toss of her head, she sent her long red tresses back off her shoulders, then lifted her face to the stars and reached out for his hands. He clasped them as she arched backward, keening and groaning as she began a feverish, rapid rocking back and forth, riding him for all he was worth. He watched her through the cleft in her breasts as she clung to his outstretched hands, huffed wildly, her tempo increasing as she rode him. And then he was telling her grimly not to stop or slow down—and then he was firing under her like a cannon. With a delighted shriek, she came also. He felt her hot juices running down his shaft. Then she collapsed forward onto his massive chest, murmuring happily as she hugged him.

"That's enough," she said softly. "For now, anyway."

"You mean," he said, still gasping, "you want more?"

"I told you. Not right away," she replied, smothering his perspiring face with kisses. "Let's wait awhile."

So that's what they did. They waited. For a while. Hawk got very little sleep that night, but surprisingly, it did not seem to bother him all that much the next day.

They remained hidden on the bluff throughout the next day, following Hawk's suggestion that they travel only by night until they put this Bannock-infested wilderness behind them. It would be safer traveling under cover of darkness, and for now, the pine-studded bluff offered excellent cover. Throughout the morning they kept themselves quiet, using a fire to cook with only at noon when there was little wind, being careful to feed it only sparingly with completely dried wood to prevent any telltale column of smoke from poking up through the pines.

It was around this noon fire that Hawk asked how Buffalo Jim knew it was Spotted Pony's Blackfoot band that had raised hell with these Bannocks. Before Jim replied, he carefully lit his clay pipe.

"A few tore-up Bannocks straggled into Fort Hall just after you left," he said. "They were hurt bad, real bad, and a brave I've done business with a few times told me what happened. He said Spotted Pony brought his people down real careful-like, surrounded at least three bands, and then—all at once, so to speak—attacked, doing his level best to wipe out every man, woman, and child. Leastways, that's how he described it to me."

Hawk frowned thoughtfully and shook his head. "That sure don't sound like the usual way Blackfoot come on their enemies. They hit and run. Steal horses. Then melt away. They never seemed all that interested in decimating their enemies like that. They don't have the organization."

Jim glanced nervously at Alice. "They do now."

"What do you mean?"

"The Bannocks saw a white man helping Spotted Pony. My guess he's Alice's brother."

Alice gasped. "James?"

"If he's with Spotted Pony, then he's the one. Tell me, ma'am, does he have any military training?"

"Yes."

"What kind?"

"West Point. He ... he didn't graduate. He was thrown out for gambling. I mean ... for not paying his gambling debts. It was a terrible scandal. He had to flee his creditors."

"That explains it, then," said Big Jim. "Spotted Pony, the most powerful chief of the Blackfoot Confederation, now has a West Point man to teach him how to wage war on his enemies."

"I don't believe this," Alice said. "It's preposterous."

"You mean you don't believe your brother would do such a thing?" Hawk asked. "Is that it?"

"That's it, exactly. He couldn't."

"Why not?"

"You mean ally himself with these savages? Become their military tutor? Not James! He would never do such a thing."

Hawk looked closely at Alice. "Maybe you can't believe he'd do it, but look at it this way, Alice: suppose he got captured by Spotted Pony's band

and saw what was in store for him if he didn't make himself valuable to the chief. And of course, all he had to sell was what he knew. Looks to me like that's what he did. He sold his knowledge of military tactics for his life. And from what I heard back at the fort, he's fitting in nicely—thinking of creating himself a kingdom all his own—with Spotted Pony's help, of course."

"And that ain't such a bad bargain, either," said Jim, leaning back and puffing on his pipe. "These here Indians know how to sneak up and rob and pillage, but they know next to nothing about long-range tactics, about really taking out an enemy for good. It's almost like they're afraid that if they don't leave a few of the enemy behind, they won't have any left for the next go-around."

Hawk nodded. "Only now it looks like the Blackfoot have got themselves a chief—and an adviser—who're going to change all that, who're willing to go all the way."

"You mean wipe out *all* their enemies?" Alice asked, her voice hushed.

Hawk glanced at her and nodded. "That's the way it looks."

Buffalo Jim removed his pipestem from his mouth and stared grimly at Alice. "And to these Blackfoot, every tribe bordering their lands is an enemy. The Crow. The Flatheads. The Shoshoni. The Bannocks. The Mandans. The Arikawa. Even, sometimes, the Gros Ventres, though right now they're allies."

Alice shuddered, then shook her head in disbelief. "I just can't see James allowing himself to be used in this way."

"Alice, why did you come out here after him?" Hawk asked.

"To bring him back."

"But how could he? You said he fled in disgrace, owing huge gambling debts."

"But I've made good on all of them—and made bribes to all the appropriate authorities. James can return now to West Point and gain his commission."

"How did you manage that?"

"It wasn't me. My Uncle Renwick died, leaving a fortune to James and myself. There's now more than enough money to put all this ugliness behind us. To start life anew. But poor James knows nothing of this. That's why I've come after him—to tell him he doesn't have to run anymore, that he can return to civilization."

Jim shook his head, the irony of the situation causing his eyes to gleam. "But don't you see, Alice? Everything's changed. For you and for him. Now that he has his own army of warriors to command and a war that could go on for a good long time, he has no need for West Point. He sees himself now as warlord of all these here Western lands."

Alice's face paled at the thought. "I certainly hope you're wrong, Jim."

"It's wild, sure enough," Hawk admitted to her, "but it does make a kind of crazy sense, Alice."

"Yes, it does, I suppose. But it is not his fault. He was treated like a criminal. Even his friends turned from him."

"Maybe that's understandable Alice. A gambler is like a drunk. He can get in so deep sometimes, he no longer has any friends—just people he gambles with."

She lowered her head. Softly she said, "I know. That's how it was for poor James." Then she forced a smile and looked up at them. "Well," she said doggedly, "I am sure when I speak to James, he'll realize how much better it will be for him to come back with me. I know James. He's no savage."

"Maybe," Jim replied as gently as he could, "and I hate to disillusion you, ma'am, but there's something I ain't told you yet."

Alice waited apprehensively.

"That white man the Bannocks saw leadin' them Blackfoot war parties had more than a few bloody scalps hanging from his belt."

Alice was aghast. She tried to speak, to protest. Then she gave it up and buried her face in her hands, horrified.

Watching her, Hawk wanted to reach over and comfort her, but he knew he had no words that could accomplish such a feat. Alice had done all she could to defend her brother before them, and it had been a gallant and praiseworthy effort— but it now seemed that the pure and simple truth of it was that even if she did reach her brother, there would be little chance she would be able to lure him back East to a civilization that had already cuffed him with such an unforgiving hand.

With Spotted Pony, he had found his niche.

Weasel Piss was pleased that Golden Hawk had apparently decided to remain in his camp throughout the day and move on again only at night. The day before, Weasel Piss had not had an easy time of it and had lost track of Golden Hawk completely until a few hours after dawn, when he came upon their camp.

His difficulty tracking Golden Hawk had been made doubly difficult by the fact that he had to evade so many Bannock parties. The Bannocks were as thick in these hills as lice on an old woman. Their several bands had been so badly mauled by the Blackfoot that they were scurrying about like ants from a destroyed anthill rushing off in all directions as they sought a new nest.

Fortunately for Weasel Piss the presence of women and children in the several Bannock parties that passed close by gave him plenty of warning, making it easy enough for him to avoid discovery. The disorganized and panicked Bannocks were filled with dismay at their terrible defeats. Having witnessed one of their battles from a safe distance, Weasel Piss could easily understand their despair. Against those well-drilled waves of Blackfoot warriors, the Bannock warriors had shown little or no staying power. They had not been defeated, they had been routed.

Still, these contemptible root-eaters remained as treacherous as ever—and Weasel Piss had not come this far to be killed by a Bannock.

Twice he had gone on his spirit quest and each time came back with only a numbing sense of emptiness and futility. The last time he lied on his return and told of a vision in which he had been carried aloft by a great eagle, but it was not long before Eagle Feather, the most powerful of the band's medicine men, had seen through his deception and soon all the tribe knew that once again he had failed to achieve a vision. Willow Tree had done nothing to hide her disapproval.

Weasel Piss had a sneaking suspicion of what the trouble was. He was different from his brother Comanches in too many ways. Taller and lankier than most of them, he bore little resemblance to these squat, bowlegged men. Furthermore, he had never been as comfortable with a horse as his peers. He rode well enough, but it was never second nature, as it was to a true Comanche. Weasel Piss was in truth a troubling aberration to himself and to his fellow braves, including his parents, both of whom were full-blooded Comanches, as unable as Weasel Piss to explain their son's odd inability to look and act like his Comanche brothers.

All Weasel Piss had left to prove himself to his fellow Kwahadi warriors was his fighting ability. Once this was established without any doubt, he would have no need, he believed, to boast of his bear brother or eagle mentor. Then would he lead others in battle, secure in the knowledge of his courage and invincibility. The treacherous Coyote Heart would be suitably chastened, Willow Tree would realize how much she wanted him for a husband, and her father would understand at last that it was not visions that counted, but action.

And now, peering through the pines at Golden Hawk and the other two huddled around the low campfire, Weasel Piss felt heady with the thought that he was now so close to achieving what had filled his dreams from the moment he had first conceived this quest. For bringing back Golden

Hawk—or his scalp—would be Weasel Piss's powerful demonstration of his worth, and in one single, bold stroke, he would accomplish all that he wished for in this life: fame, justification . . . and Willow Tree as his wife.

The hunchback was smoking his pipe. Golden Hawk was cleaning his rifle. The white woman had curled up on a blanket on the far side of the barely flickering campfire. Weasel Piss could not be sure, but the girl appeared to be asleep. The hunchback and Golden Hawk were talking quietly, so quietly the Indian could not hear a sound.

It was late in the afternoon and clear to Weasel Piss that if he were to strike, it would have to be now, before they set off again that night. His plan was simple and direct: an arrow would impale the hunchbacked one, and a second later Weasel Piss would launch himself through the air, catching Golden Hawk about the shoulders and slamming him back off the bluff. When they crashed finally to the brush below, Golden Hawk would be so stunned, perhaps even unconscious, that Weasel Piss would have no difficulty disarming or killing him. The hunchback would be no threat to him, and he could simply ignore the white woman. Like all of her kind, she would simply occupy herself screaming in terror.

Raising slowly to a crouch, Weasel Piss fitted the arrow to his bowstring and swiftly drew it back.

—4—

A few moments before, his attention apparently on his rifle, Hawk did not look up as Buffalo Jim casually knocked the tobacco from his pipe and said, "You recognize that Bannock, hoss?"

"He ain't a Bannock, Jim."

"What is he, then?"

"Comanche. The war paint and headband. Kwahadi. It's me he's after."

"After *you*? My God," whispered Alice from the ground where she huddled, Hawk's huge revolver in her hand. "Aren't you going to do anything?"

"I'm doing it—waiting for the son of a bitch to make his move." As Hawk spoke, his lips barely moved. "Just lie quiet and stay out of this—if you can."

As casually as possible, Hawk put his rifle down and eased his bowie from its sheath, while Jim reached for the handle of his hatchet stuck in his belt. Out of the corner of his eye, Hawk watched the Comanche brave slowly part the brush in front of him as he leaned forward to study them more closely.

"He's gettin' ready to make his move," whispered Jim.

"I can see him," Hawk whispered.

Abruptly, Hawk saw the Comanche fitting his arrow to the bowstring.

"Duck!" Hawk told Jim.

But the arrow was already in flight, sounding like the wings of a small bird. The arrow struck him high on his hump with enough force to knock him violently back, his cry drowned out by the fierce war cry of the Comanche as he flung himself the few remaining yards at Hawk.

Hawk stood up to meet the Comanche's charge. The Indian slammed into him shoulder-high and sent him reeling backward as Alice, her eyes closed in terror, fired up at the Comanche as he catapulted past her. Hawk smelled the sour sweat of the Indian's body as it struck him, and thrust up with his bowie. As he toppled back off the bluff, he felt the blade sinking into muscle.

Hawk tumbled backward into space, the Comanche sticking to him like a leech. He struck a shelf of gravel, shoulder-first. It gave way under him and the back of his head struck a projecting rock. Daggers of pain exploded deep inside his skull. The Comanche still wrapped about him, Hawk continued to tumble down the steep slope, reaching out frantically for shrubs or pine shoots to grab. But he was tumbling too fast.

The tops of spruce trees rushed up at him. He struck the ground hard again, then felt himself once more launched into space. The earth exchanged places with the sky. He struck the slope again, his head and shoulders slamming deep into the soft shale and gravel, the Comanche's weight drilling him deeper into the ground. He turned completely over twice before coming to a sudden, shattering halt—his head spinning crazily, his entire body numb.

The Comanche, knocked loose, cartwheeled past Hawk down the rest of the slope, then slammed into a thick clump of junipers. Hawk saw him twist about as he came to a halt and look back up at him with a grim, singleness of purpose the fall had not altered. The bowie still in his hand, Hawk pushed himself to his feet and plunged swiftly down the rest of the slope and into the junipers after the Comanche.

The Comanche was waiting, crouched, an upraised hatchet in his hand. There was a raw, bleeding gash in his side where Hawk's blade had entered, and a long, raw-looking gash on the Comanche's forehead that resembled a brand—and Hawk remembered suddenly Alice firing up at the Comanche.

"Who the hell are you?" he snarled in Comanche at the crouching warrior.

"I am Weasel Piss."

"I thought I recognized the stench."

Hawk charged. But his right foot came down on a loose pocket of shale, and he plunged awkwardly forward to the ground just as the Comanche came down with his hatchet, missing Hawk's skull by inches. Reaching up, Hawk grabbed the Comanche's wrist and yanked him to the ground beside him. Then he rolled over onto him. As he brought up his bowie to bury it into the savage's heart, the Comanche caught Hawk's wrist with both hands and, gathering his feet under him, pushed upward.

A profound weakness was rapidly falling over Hawk, and he found himself unable to prevent himself from being propelled backward. His back slammed into a tree. He slashed out at the Comanche, catching him in the chest. As the blade sliced in past a rib, the Comanche cried out and spun away, pulling the knife from Hawk's grasp. Blood gushing from his second wound, the Comanche vanished into the brush. Snatching up the bowie, Hawk lurched after him, as unsteady on his feet as any drunken Indian after a trading session. Hawk kept on after the Comanche, nevertheless, chasing the sound he made crashing through the timber ahead of him.

Hawk became dimly aware of the sound of swift water close by, but gave it no heed as he plunged on after the Comanche. The ground rose under his feet. The Comanche was leading him higher into the timber. That the wounded Comanche could still move this fast did not discourage him, and he kept on doggedly, despite his bone-deep weariness. Perspiration broke out all over him, stinging his eyes and nearly blinding him. He felt himself step into a patch of thick pine needles and dried twigs. There was a sharp, cracking sound as a thatch of dried branches gave way under his foot. He plunged through and saw a stream bank rushing up at him. Glancing off the embankment, he slid into the icy water and was immediately swept along in the swift current.

He struggled, not to swim, but just to keep his head above water as he felt his body flung into the narrow channel between two large rocks, the growing roar of rapids filling the universe with sound. Then he was dragged under the surface and pulled rapidly along. Gasping for air, he felt himself plastered against a huge boulder. It blocked his passage until the current plucked him off and sent him past it.

His progress was swifter now, and not at all gentle. Carried along with the current, he was dropping rapidly, skimming over rocks, at times slamming into them with numbing force. When he tried to gain some control over his progress, he found he was completely drained, as weak as a kitten. For a moment he was on the surface, gasping for breath, sucking in great lungfuls of air. Glancing up, he caught sight of a patch of blue sky—and standing on a distant rise what appeared to be Alice and Jim peering down at him.

With ruthless indifference, the water snatched him out of sight around another boulder and he found himself plunging headfirst over a falls at least twenty feet high. Knifing into the pool beneath it, he narrowly missed a huge granite chunk at the base of the falls. A swift undertow caught him and dragged him deeper and still deeper, the icy waters closing about him like a vise. Only gradually did the churning and buffeting coming from above fade. The undertow slackened slightly. But the terrible, paralyzing cold had sapped him of all volition and he made no effort to help himself as he began drifting down, twisting slowly as he fell away from the distant light glimmering on the surface above. He kept on sinking—like something completely spent.

Or dead.

That thought alarmed him. He turned and began to pull himself through the leaden waters toward the light. The pain in his oxygen-starved lungs was excruciating, and no matter how hard he pulled toward the light above him, it seemed to get no closer. But he would not give up. He could not. Furious that he had allowed that damned Comanche to do this to him, he began to kick upward. It seemed like an eternity, but was probably only seconds before his head broke free of the encasing waters.

Sucking in huge gulps of air, he struck out for the boulder-strewn embankment less than twenty feet away and before long managed to haul himself up onto the bank, surprised to find he was still clutching his bowie. Sheathing it, he staggered into a nearby stand of alders.

He realized he did not have the strength to go much farther. Aware now of a steady throbbing in the back of his head, he put his hand back to feel it. He was surprised at the depth of the gash running across the back of his skull and the heavy carapace of dried blood below it. He must have lost a considerable amount of blood, he realized. No wonder his limbs had turned to lead. Fortunately, the near-frigid cold of the mountain stream had apparently stemmed the blood's flow—for now, at least.

Without bothering to remove his heavy, sopping-wet garments, he stretched out full-length on the ground and dropped at once into an exhausted sleep.

Weasel Piss made it back to his horse by noon the next day. The two knife wounds had slowed him considerably and he was feverish. His right side was on fire, his chest cavity so filled with blood he could barely suck air into his lungs. He was pleased at the gunshot wound, aware that it would mark his forehead forever, reminding all who looked upon him that it was he who had captured or taken the scalp of the mighty Golden Hawk. It would give him a new name: Scarface. Yes. He liked that better than Weasel Piss. Much better.

After pulling himself onto his waiting pony, he rode back to the bluff, dismounted, and carefully approached the campsite where he had surprised Golden Hawk. He found it deserted, recovered his bow and quiver, returned to his pony, and rode south toward the Snake, keeping high in the timbered slopes until he emerged into the foothills three days later near Golden Hawk's cabin. He had visited it a week earlier. Finding it deserted, he had ridden to Fort Hall, where he had learned that Golden Hawk had left not long before, and the direction he had taken.

Now, once more approaching Golden Hawk's cabin, he found himself riding around the flanks of a towering escarpment and came upon titanic boulders and slabs of rock that had peeled off the rock face and now made a huge pile at its base. It was dark. Too weary to go any farther, he made camp by a spring he found in among the boulders.

Despite his two wounds, which were not healing as well as he would have expected, he built himself a fire and managed to bring down a rabbit with his bow. He roasted the rabbit over a makeshift spit, ate it with gusto, and then curled up in his blanket close by the fire. So exhausted was he that he fell asleep almost the moment his head touched the ground.

The restless pawing and skittish snorting of his pony awakened him. His pony was obviously in great distress and Weasel Piss could hear it pulling desperately on its tether. Then the shattering snarl of a great cat coming from the rocks just above him caused him to leap to his feet. An enormous male mountain cat was crouched on a rock slab above the campfire's still-glowing embers, his long tail whipping smoothly back and forth.

For an unnerving moment Weasel Piss hoped that his suffering of the past few days had presented him finally with a vision. But the glow of the cougar's eyes in the darkness, a second snarling roar, and most important of all his unmistakable smell brought the trembling Comanche back to reality. This was not the product of a starved and tortured mind, but a living creature all too real . . . and all too dangerous.

With a cold, sober clarity, Weasel Piss knew what he had to do. As sweat broke out on his forehead, he reached for his bow and quiver, noticing as he did the condition of the cougar's right thigh. It was puckered and shrunken from an old wound. As a result, the cat's right leg was barely able to support his right side. This crippled old cat was having a rough time feeding itself, Weasel Piss realized, and was reduced to feeding on slow, more easily taken game. Like stock. And people.

The cat snarled softly, then tipped his head and lowered it, moving stealthily to the edge of the rock. In a moment he would spring. His bow

in his left hand, an arrow in his right, Weasel
Piss ducked back behind a boulder. The cat
bounded off the rock, whipped around the boulder, and turned to face Weasel Piss. As the cat
gathered himself to pounce, Weasel Piss lifted
his bow and let fly. He had aimed for the throat,
but his aim was poor, and the shaft buried itself
in the cougar's right shoulder, striking nothing
vital. The cat snarled in pain, turned, and leapt
away into the night.

Weasel Piss slumped back against a boulder
and fitted another arrow to his bow.

The night was shattered by the sudden, almost
human squealing of his pony. Dashing through
the darkness toward the sound, he came upon the
big cat astride the pony's quivering flank. The
pony was still alive, its head thrashing, its eyes
starting out of its head, streams of lather hanging
from its muzzle. The cat looked up at the approaching Comanche, snarled a warning, then
bent his head as he resumed feeding inside the
great rent he had opened in the pony's gut.
The arrow Weasel Piss had buried in the cougar's shoulder was still visible.

With trembling hands Weasel Piss lifted his
bow and let the shaft fly. It glanced harmlessly
off the pony's backbone, and before Weasel Piss
could fit another arrow to his bowstring, the
cougar—trailing a long rope of steaming entrails
from his mouth—vanished into the night.

But not without one final, malevolent glance
back over his shoulder at Weasel Piss.

Returning to his camp, Weasel Piss gathered
up his things, and leaving the ravaged pony as a
reluctant offering to that fearsome cat, he con-

tinued on through the night. Close to dawn he reached Golden Hawk's empty cabin. He kicked open the door. Standing in the gloom of its interior, he heard the scuttering of tiny feet as chipmunks and field mice ran for their holes. The unclean stench of the white man assaulted his nostrils.

Staying inside a white man's cabin had not been his intention. Certain that Golden Hawk would return to his lodge before winter, Weasel Piss had planned to wait for his return in the timber within sight of the cabin. But the thought of that great, malevolent beast prowling about convinced him it would be wise to shelter himself in the cabin, during the nights at least.

Feverish and unable to breathe without pain, he realized he would need weeks to regain his strength. The moment he thought this, he felt what strength remained drained away—like water in sand. He pushed the door shut firmly behind him and collapsed shakily to the floor. Without bothering to throw a blanket over himself, he slept.

When Hawk finally awakened after pulling himself from the stream, he found that a full day had passed and that he was not alone. A very old Nez Percé Indian was squatting beside him, studying his face intently while his pony cropped the grass behind him. Hawk sat up. His heavy buckskins, sopping wet when he collapsed, now encased his arms and legs in an icy grip.

Hawk peeled out of his shirt and britches as the Nez Percé Indian got up and took a blanket from his parfleche bag and offered it to Hawk.

Hawk's Nez Percé was about as good as his Shoshoni, serviceable but not very eloquent. In the Nez Percé tongue he thanked the old man as he wrapped the blanket around his trembling shoulders and loins.

"How are you called?" he asked the old warrior.

"Tames Horses."

"That's a nice pony you got there."

"He is old horse. But from his balls come many fine ponies."

"What you doing out here, chief? This here's Bannock country."

"I have no people now. I am like old buffalo who stand outside the herd and wait for the wolves to pull him down."

"I think it will take more than wolves to bring you down, chief," Hawk commented, shivering.

"I will build fire," Tames Horses told him.

"Careful, chief. There's Bannock all around."

"I am not afraid of the Bannock." Tames Horses smiled then, revealing impressively white, healthy teeth. "This would be a good day to die."

"Maybe for you, chief. But I got things to do before I die. Many things."

Tames Horses shrugged and moved off to gather firewood. Before long he had a warm, nearly smokeless campfire going and over it two fat rabbits turning on a spit. To bring down the small game, the old chief hadn't used his flintlock, only his bow and two arrows, and hadn't been gone more than a few minutes. If he was on his last legs, Hawk remarked to himself, it sure as hell didn't look like it.

"Chief," Hawk said, tearing eagerly into a juicy, succulent rabbit leg, "there ain't no Nez Percé

Indian band foolish enough to let go of a chief with your talents."

"This is true," the old Indian admitted calmly. "But my people do not send me from them. I go myself."

"Why's that, chief?"

"Because my woman die of the spotted sickness and my two sons do not return from raiding party. Then I see it is time for me to go alone into these hills, to flee the stench of other men, even that of my red brothers. And it was good I do this. These trees and this pine-scented wind has cleaned my soul. Now I think I go back to my people. But not right away." The old man looked searchingly at Hawk. "And what about your sons and your woman?"

"I have no sons."

"And no woman?"

"She's with her people, the Crow. She is very sick, mauled by a cougar—a mankiller."

"Such cougar's are very dangerous. To them a human being is very easy game. And his flesh is very sweet—for this maybe he go a little crazy." The chief shook his head, the wind lifting his thinning white hair slightly. "And what about your parents? Where are they?"

"Gone, like dead flowers on the wind, old man. The Comanches kill them many years ago, then take my sister and me."

The old Indian's face showed no emotion at these words. "Which Comanches?"

"The Kwahadi."

Tames Horses nodded. "A remote people. They have fine horses, but not as fine as the Nez Percé. It is as I thought when I saw you asleep on the ground. You are the white man they call Golden Hawk, the great warrior so many brave warriors have lost their breath seeking. It is said you are on speaking terms with the Great Cannibal Owl."

Hawk shrugged. "That's what they say, chief."

"I do not believe in the Great Cannibal Owl."

"Neither do I."

"That is strange."

"But I find it useful if my enemies do."

The old warrior's wrinkled face did not smile, but his eyes did. "At least you are not an iron heart."

"Iron heart?"

"They are the many white settlers who travel through the Nez Percé land without their parents. I ask them where their old people are. They say they leave them in the land back East. The hearts of these people are made of iron."

"Perhaps the old parents they leave behind do not wish to make such a long and difficult journey."

"Then the settlers should not leave them to journey to these lands. It would be better if they stay home anyway. Now they cut wide trails through the Nez Percé land and frighten away the game. But you are not an iron heart. You do not scare away the game. And you are a very famous warrior."

Hawk smiled at the old Indian. "Thanks, chief."

"I am not chief now. But many summers ago I was great war chief and take many scalps. My name rang with renown and my enemies were legion. I think that was the foolishness of youth.

Now I am not a chief. But you may call me chief if you wish."

The meal was over. It had been a good one, the food kindling a warmth deep inside him. His conversation with the chief had built a like fire in his heart. The icy chill that had enclosed him since he had awakened was gone completely now.

Earlier, a quick examination of Hawk's head wound revealed that a tough scab had already formed, though the wound itself and the area around it were quite tender to his touch. Hawk guessed that the icy-water had reduced the swelling, and so far there was no sign of an infection.

Before the meal, Hawk had spread his still-damp clothing on top of some boulders along the bank of the stream. By noon they were dry enough for him to wear, and as soon as he was dressed, the two men—Tames Horses riding, Hawk walking beside him—set out for the bluff where Hawk had left Alice and Big Jim.

His hope—a forlorn one at best—was that he would find them waiting for him. But he realized that this was highly unlikely. From that glimpse they had gained of him as he was being swept along into the rapids, it must have seemed obvious that Hawk was a gone beaver and that the only course open to them now was to continue on under cover of darkness as they had planned.

Hawk had tethered his horse by a stream not far from the bluff. It was no longer there. Buffalo Jim had taken it as a spare packhorse, no doubt. Good thinking on his part, Hawk realized, but as a result, he was now afoot.

Standing beside Hawk, Tames Horses bent to pluck a long grass stem.

"What do you now, Hawk?"

"It beats the shit out of me, chief."

"You need pony."

"That's what I need, all right. And my rifle and sidearm. Both of them are on the way to Spotted Pony's camp."

"That is long way from here. Nez Percé not welcome, I think, in Spotted Pony's camp. Neither is Golden Hawk."

"I was counting on Alice Cantrell's influence with her brother to keep me out of trouble."

"This white woman and the buffalo man, they are not far ahead, I think."

"True. So long, chief."

"You go now?"

"I got to get a move on if I'm going to overtake my friends."

"I will give you my pony. He is old, but has a good, strong heart. He will not fail you."

"Thanks, chief. I really appreciate that. But you keep the pony."

The chief paused and held up his hand to silence Hawk. Hawk glanced quickly around and saw a mounted Bannock broke from the alders behind them about thirty yards distant. Turning in the other direction, Hawk saw a second Bannock break from the trees lining the stream and head toward them.

Hawk and Tames Horses were afoot and would have to stand and fight.

"What do you want to do, chief? Run?"

The old chief's teeth flashed in his dark, wrinkled face. "Beats the shit out of me."

The two Bannocks booted their ponies into a hard gallop, filling the air with their war cries. One held a hatchet over his head, the other a stone war club. Hawk readied himself for the one charging directly at him, assuming Tames Horses would take the other. Neither had time to discuss the matter.

Lunging close to the Bannock's horse, Hawk reached up for the band holding up the warrior's breechclout. The Bannock swung his club, the heavy stone glancing painfully off Hawk's shoulder as Hawk hauled back on the Bannock's waistband and dragged the Indian from his saddle.

The Bannock landed on his back, momentarily stunned. Hawk drew his bowie and plunged it into the Bannock's chest. The Indian struggled for a moment, a thin stream of blood running from the corner of his mouth; then he lay back, his body convulsing. Hawk withdrew the knife and turned to see how Tames Horses was doing.

Not so well. The Bannock was on top of the chief, and Tames Horses had only his bloody forearm to ward him off. As the Bannock raised his hatchet, Hawk reached back behind his neck and threw his throwing knife. Its tumbling blade plunged into the Bannock's neck. Clasping his throat in an effort to stem the sudden freshet of blood, the Bannock toppled off Tames Horses.

Hawk hurried over to the warrior's slowly twisting body and removed his throwing knife. Wiping off the blade, he turned his attention to Tames Horses. The old warrior was sitting up, examining his right arm. The Bannock's hatchet had sliced through the skin of his forearm, shattering the bone. The single shard protruded through the purpling flesh, like the fang of a snarling dog. The bone would need to be set, then bound with splints.

"We don't have much time," Hawk reminded him. "These hills are lousy with Bannocks."

"Yes. And now we both have ponies. We will ride out of these hills and put the Bannocks behind us."

"You can't ride with an arm like that. It's broken."

"It is of no matter. Go now and ride to overtake your friends."

Hawk shook his head. "I will stay with you. There will be time for them later. Right now, I'd better set that bone and fashion a splint for it."

Hawk hurried off, cut splints from saplings, and quickly returned. He found the old chief waiting for him calmly, having already set the compound fracture himself. Hawk probed the swollen, discolored arm to make sure the join was a good one, then carefully bound the splints around it with strips of rawhide he found in the Indian's parfleche. The rawhide strips he sprinkled lightly with water before winding them about the splint, so they would tighten the splints more snugly about the broken arm when they dried.

Hawk stepped back, satisfied with his crude cast. It would hold, he was sure. The old warrior's wrinkled face was pale, as if all of the Indian had been drained from it. But his anthracite eyes had lost none of their power, and without a word, he got to his feet and walked toward one of the two ponies they had just won in battle.

"On this root-eater's pony I will ride back to

the bluff," he told Hawk. "You ride the other one."

Before Hawk could help him, the old chief swung onto the Bannock's pony and started off. Hawk caught the reins of the second Bannock pony, mounted up, and urged it after Tames Horses.

Hawk had found a brave man to ride with—all the way to Spotted Pony's camp, if it came to that.

—— 5 ——

As they continued north toward the Powder River, Hawk decided it was time to do something about Tames Horses' arm. It did not look good. And though for the past three days the old warrior had uttered not a single word of complaint, Hawk knew he was in constant pain. Whenever anything—a trailing branch, a horse's flank, a rein even—came in direct contact with his swollen right forearm, he closed his eyes momentarily in a silent, stoic acknowledgment of his discomfort.

They made camp by a spring well-hidden in a heavy stand of spruce, the ground carpeted with pine needles, the air redolent with their scent. It was midday but Hawk announced they were going to remain where they were until he thoroughly examined Tames Horses' arm.

Tames Horses did not argue as Hawk cut away the rawhide holding the splint in place. Even before he had cut off the last of it and peeled away the splints, he saw the purplish, inflamed flesh where the bone splinter had broken through. A raging infection had set in. Judging from the smell, it was probably gangrene. One thing at least the chief could be grateful for: it would be the more deadly gangrene left by a bullet wound.

"It looks like the bone's setting all right," Hawk told the chief, "but I'll have to open up the arm."

The Indian shrugged.

"And cauterize it."

Tames Horses said nothing, his black eyes inscrutable. A moment later, using the tip of his bowie, Hawk slit open the arm, let the infection drain, then brought the chief over to the spring. The water in the pool under it was ice-cold, and Hawk washed the wound out in it. This done, he built a fire and held the blade of his bowie in the flames until it was white-hot, then laid the flat blade into the wound. The stench of singed flesh assailed his nostrils as he ranged the blade still farther in so as to cauterize all the diseased flesh. Withdrawing the knife, he glanced at the chief.

His eyes were closed and it looked as if he were asleep. But he wasn't. As Hawk pulled back, he got slowly to his feet and walked on steady legs back over to the pool, sat calmly beside it, and again lowered his arm into its icy depths. When it was practically numb from the cold, he withdrew it and walked over to a tree and sat under it. Leaning his head back against the tree, he held his arm out for Hawk to bandage once again.

"Not yet," Hawk told him. "Wait here, chief. I'm going to find something to make a poultice with."

"Good." The Indian closed his eyes. "I will rest."

Mounting up, Hawk rode out, ranging for miles

before he found the mold he was looking for in a damp, shaded spot under a fallen pine. As he was digging it up with his knife, he heard a distant whinny and then the dim thunder of many hoofbeats. Carefully packing the mold into one of his saddlebags, he rode on through the timber toward the sound he had heard, and less than a mile later he came out onto a heavily wooded ridge overlooking a long river valley. Dismounting, he moved closer to the edge of the timber to get a clearer view. The river below him was the Musselshell. On both sides of it, stretching away for as far as the eye could see, were gently rolling hills, thinly wooded, covered for the most part with lush, sun-bronzed, hip-high grasses undulating in the wind.

Lined along the river's banks were Bannock tepees, most of them with ponies tethered in front. Hawk counted at least sixty, perhaps seventy, lodges in all, and in the lush fields some distance farther down the river the Bannocks' large pony herd was grazing. In the shallow water along the banks Hawk saw Bannock women washing clothes. Nearly naked boys ran in raucous play through the camp, and Bannock braves—old and young—walked idly about or squatted on blankets, more than likely gambling or telling stories.

It was a peaceful scene—except for one very disquieting fact.

On the wooded slope directly below Hawk a sizable host of mounted Blackfoot warriors were waiting to attack. Like Hawk, they were hidden in a screen of thick timber.

When this signal to attack would come Hawk

had no idea, but what impressed him the most and sent a cold shiver of apprehension up his spine was the incredible discipline shown by that silent multitude of mounted Blackfoot Indians waiting below him dressed for battle, their lances at salute, their ponies as motionless as their riders.

Moving cautiously back to his horse, Hawk placed his hand over its mouth to prevent it from whinnying, and moved back off the ridge and deep into the timber. Then he led his horse up a steep slope until he gained a better view of the entire river valley.

Drifting up from the Bannock village far below him came the sound of women's laughter, faint but unmistakable. Hawk heard clearly the shrill outcry of the youngsters at play. Lazy columns of wood smoke drifted skyward from many of the lodges. Completely unaware of their traditional Blackfoot enemy waiting to sweep down on them, the Bannocks went peacefully about their business. A quiet day was apparently winding down to another quiet, peaceful night.

When? Hawk asked himself in an agony of apprehension. When would the signal to attack be given?

And then he saw movement on the crest of a distant knoll on the far side of the river, followed by the wink of sunlight on metal. Two horsemen rode into view. Shading his eyes, Hawk saw that one of the riders was a Blackfoot chief, resplendent in a long, trailing eagle-feather headdress. The other rider was a buckskin-clad white man wearing a large, floppy-brimmed hat. At his side a saber hung in its scabbard. It was the saber's highly polished hilt that Hawk had seen flashing in the sun.

He had found Alice Cantrell's brother.

Now he knew who was responsible for those silent, disciplined ranks of Blackfoot Indians waiting below him. As Hawk watched, Cantrell withdrew his saber from its scabbard and held it straight out for a moment, then let it fall. Instantly a small mounted force of Blackfoot warriors—no more than ten, Hawk judged—burst from the timber and charged across the flat toward the Bannock village.

Emitting shrill, piercing war cries, the Blackfoot warriors made no effort to hide their approach. Screaming, the Bannock women bolted from the banks along the river and ran for the protection of their camp, while the Bannock braves wasted no time mounting their ponies and rode out eagerly to do battle. The Blackfoot attack must have appeared to them as foolhardy, even suicidal. They could see at once the small size of the attacking force and were obviously delighted to take advantage of their enemy's apparent foolhardiness.

Once the hard-charging Blackfoot force had drawn the Bannock warriors from the village, however, they did not engage the Bannocks; they veered away from the encampment instead, giving every indication that they had lost heart when they saw the mounted Bannocks charging toward them from the village. Down the river valley they fled, drawing the yelping Bannock braves after them. From where he stood, Hawk could hear the distant pop of rifle and pistol fire. The Blackfoot warriors had swift ponies—undoubtedly the best Spotted Pony could provide—and they had no difficulty keeping the eagerly pursuing Bannocks just out of reach. Then, gradually, the Blackfoot warriors described a slow circle until they were racing back up the flat, the howling Bannocks still on their tail. Pursued and pursuers passed between the village and the slope and kept coming, the Blackfoot force deliberately slowing now, drawing the foolish Bannocks still deeper into the trap.

Hawk had a chilling awareness of the Bannocks' fate by now and for a fleeting instant wanted to shout a warning or send a shot into the air. But the curtain had already risen. The characters were on stage. Nothing could stop this tragedy from unfolding to its inevitable, grim conclusion.

As the yelping Bannocks flashed past just below him, Hawk glanced across the river in time to see the man he was certain was James Cantrell raise his saber over his head. For an instant the gleaming blade hung in the air. Then, like the fabled Sword of Damocles, it flashed down.

Out from the timber exploded the remaining Blackfoot warriors. Reaching the flat, they split into two columns, one of which headed for the Bannock village while the other charged after the Bannocks, overtook them, and slammed into their unprotected flanks. With perfect precision, the original Blackfoot force spun about to engage the Bannock force from the front ... and in that moment the trap snapped shut. The Bannock warriors, which only a few minutes before had ridden out of the village with bloodthirsty enthusiasm, now found themselves milling helplessly inside the jaws of a rapidly closing pincers. Within a few brief minutes the Blackfoot warriors began cutting them to pieces.

By this time the third column of Blackfoot warriors had reached the village. Shrill cries pierced the air. Hawk saw tepees blossoming into flames and women being dragged behind mounted Blackfoot warriors. He glimpsed old men and women pursued by mounted Blackfoot, then overtaken, to be cut down by arrows or impaled on lances.

Incredibly, through all this, a small group of Bannocks managed to fight their way out of the village through the hard-charging ranks of Blackfoot, while some of them kept up a murderous rear-guard action that allowed many of the Bannocks to escape across the flat into the timber.

But these were, at best, only pitiful remnants of the Bannock band. The majority of the village's defenders were being cut down with a sickening, ruthless thoroughness, and before long the devastation of the Bannock village was complete as a few Blackfoot warriors broke from it and rode down the bank of the river to circle the Bannock pony herd. In a short while they had driven them north toward a distant, timbered ridge. Meanwhile, the village was in flames, what remained of its lodges and winter provisions pumping into the air in great columns of black smoke.

Now, with the battle over, those Bannock warriors on the ground still living were lanced and mutilated with a grim ferocity, while old men and those women and children caught before they could flee were rounded up to be led into a tight circle beside the stream. Their fate was uncertain, Hawk realized. Some of the women, if strong enough, would be brought back to the Blackfoot camp as slaves; the children, if not too old, would be absorbed into the Blackfoot ranks. Meanwhile, Hawk watched with mounting horror as the triumphant Blackfoot warriors rode back and forth through the village, searching out and dispatching any Bannock men, young or old, they found still alive.

Glancing back at the distant knoll, Hawk saw Spotted Pony and James Cantrell move off it and begin to descend the long slope toward the village. They seemed to be in no hurry. There was no reason why they should be. The battle was over and a detested enemy of the Blackfoot had been decimated. From such a crushing defeat, this particular band could never hope to recover. What survivors there were would have to be absorbed by other Bannock bands, if they were lucky enough to find such. Spotted Pony had made excellent use of James Cantrell's West Point experience.

Hawk had seen enough. More than enough.

He hurried back to his mount and stepped onto his saddle. As he wheeled his horse and started back down the slope, he heard the rapid, staccato beat of unshod hooves and, glancing up, saw two Blackfoot warriors breaking from the timber on his right. They had probably been sent by Cantrell and Spotted Pony to round up any fleeing Bannocks. Though Hawk didn't much resemble a Bannock brave, that evidently made little difference to these Blackfoot warriors. To them, anyone not a Blackfoot was fair game.

Hawk's rifle and Colt were with Alice and Jim, which left him with only his bowie and his throwing knife. Turning his mount quickly, Hawk spurred directly for the two Blackfoot. This unexpected frontal assault momentarily confused them, and at the last moment they veered apart. Hawk left his saddle in a flying leap and slammed into the Blackfoot on his right, catching him shoulder-high and knocking him backward off his pony.

The Indian slammed into the ground beneath him. Hawk heard the sudden explosion of air from his lungs. At the same time he plunged the bowie into the Blackfoot's chest, then leapt to his feet in time to take the mounted charge of the second Blackfoot. The pony's chest crashed into Hawk, knocking him to the ground. He rolled over and found he had lost his bowie. Before he could reach back under his hair for his throwing knife, the Blackfoot flung himself from his horse, crunching into Hawk, his face a hellish mask of fury as he slammed Hawk about the head and shoulders with his stone war club.

Hawk backed up grimly, his forearms upraised and neck hunched to protect himself from the brutal rain of blows. At last, feigning exhaustion, he dropped to one knee. The Blackfoot lunged in closer, eager now to finish him off, opening himself up as he did so. Hawk flung himself at the Indian's knees, cutting him down. The Indian toppled back, his war club dropping from his grasp; over and over the two rolled as each attempted to gain an advantage over the other.

Momentarily atop the Blackfoot, Hawk felt a loose branch under one hand, snatched it up, and slammed the Blackfoot repeatedly on the side of his head. The ruthless battering took almost immediate effect as blood exploded from the Blackfoot's ear and a bright stream issued from a nostril. Hawk flung away the club and sat back, sucking in great lungfuls of air. He glanced over at the other Blackfoot. He was still on his back. Pushing himself upright was not easy, but once Hawk could stand unaided, he walked over and looked down at the Blackfoot. He was breathing still and might recover. At that moment Hawk could have killed the Blackfoot warrior, taken his scalp. But Hawk had seen too much of that sort of thing this afternoon.

He looked about for his horse and saw it calmly cropping the grass at its feet about forty yards down the slope. Retrieving his bowie knife, he wiped the blade clean in the grass and went after his horse.

Hawk had fought hard—with a resolute fury born of the knowledge that unless he got back to Tames Horses with the mold he had found, there was a good chance the old chief would die. For Hawk was convinced that only a poultice made from this mold would be capable of drawing the remaining poison from the infected forearm, and that, if this treatment failed, there was little chance he would be able to save Tames Horses' arm—or his life.

When Hawk arrived back at the camp where he had left the old chief, he found him asleep with his head back against the trunk of a pine. Dismounting, he watched Tames Horses wake up slowly, opening his liquid black eyes and gazing up at him wonderingly, as if he had never expected to see him again. Indeed, his pleasure at the sight of Hawk standing before him was so readily apparent, his joy was almost childlike.

"How's the arm?" Hawk asked as he opened his saddlebag and took out the funky-smelling mold.

The Indian looked at the mold Hawk was holding carefully in both hands. "It is better now, I think. What are you going to do with that nest of spiders?"

"Make a poultice from it and wrap it around your arm. I know it sounds crazy, but this mold will draw all that poison out. You'll know it for sure when you begin to feel it getting itchy."

"I think maybe the cold water again will be enough."

"Trust me."

"Golden Hawk is now a medicine man?"

"When I was with the Kwahadi, a captured Zuni showed me how this mold works. If I could have found a yarrow plant, I might have used that instead. This will have to do."

The Indian shrugged and let Hawk do what he wanted. Sprinkling the mold slightly with water from the spring, Hawk moistened it to the consistency of mud, then pressed the mold into the long, ugly wound, carefully covering the mold in turn with fresh pine needles, which he bound tightly about the arm with rawhide. When he was done, he used the remaining rawhide to fashion a sling.

Relieved that he had, for now, done all he could, Hawk stepped back to survey his handiwork. Tames Horses seemed cautiously pleased with the way his arm felt and pronounced himself fit to travel.

"Tomorrow," Hawk told him. "Not now. It is getting late. You need to rest up and I want to build our campfire well before dark."

Hawk did not explain this last to Tames Horses, but he saw from the look in the Indian's eyes that no explanation was needed. By dusk the campfire was out and the two had finished their coffee and were sitting in the gloom, pipes in hand, sucking the tobacco smoke deep into their lungs.

At last Hawk took the pipe from his mouth. "I have much to tell you," he said to Tames Horses.

"Your face already tells me much."

Frowning, Hawk felt of his swollen cheekbone. It was quite tender. Exploring further, his fingers found a ridged abrasion on the point of his chin. At once Hawk found himself remembering with painful vividness the Blackfoot warrior's cruel war club. Now that he thought of it, his shoulder and neck seemed to get more tender by the minute; he had no doubt that if he removed his shirt, he would find his shoulders and neck were a mass of purplish welts and bruises.

"I did not find Alice Cantrell and Buffalo Jim. But I found Spotted Pony and James Cantrell, Alice's brother."

"They did not greet you like brothers, I see."

"It wasn't them did this. On the way back here, I was overtaken by two Blackfoot warriors."

"You killed them?"

"One of them for sure—but I did not take any scalps."

"Instead, you left them for the vultures? Their

ghosts will not rest. They will wander in the land between this one and the Sand Hills."

Hawk shrugged. "I saw enough scalping for one day."

"Tell me about it."

Hawk described the battle he had witnessed and James Cantrell's part in it. When he had finished, Tames Horses looked away from Hawk, his eyes troubled.

"What you say fills me with dread. The Indian sees in battle a chance for glory. To gain this glory he will be just as happy to steal a warrior's prized pony from in front of his lodge as to take that warrior's scalp in battle. To be courageous in battle, to ride well, and to return with many stories to prove his courage—this is why the red man fights. And of course to impress his woman. But he does not fight to die. And he does not really wish to wipe out and massacre all his enemies."

"Why not?"

"Because then he will have no more enemies. The game will be over. It would be a sad time indeed if spring comes and he has no enemies to insult, no pony herds to plunder, and no more tales to tell around the winter fires."

"There were sure as hell very few Bannock left after Spotted Pony's attack. And it came without warning. The Bannocks had no chance. It was like lifting a stone and stepping on a nest of ants."

"It is the way the white man fights. To win forever."

"Guess that's it, all right."

Tames Horses shook his head. "I do not like

this. Spotted Pony and his Blackfoot band have often boasted they will wipe out the Crow and the Shoshoni, and all their other enemies. But for the Blackfoot, any tribe that hunts the buffalo becomes enemies of the Blackfoot. They are fools, I think. But dangerous fools. Like some white faces, they think they own the world because they ride upon it."

Hawk nodded. The Blackfoot were a hard and unforgiving people, all right. Their confederation had stopped the Crows solid and had even kept the Sioux and the northern Cheyenne from moving into the high plains. Now, with this white man to help them, this rogue West Point officer, they would become even more of a threat to their neighboring tribes.

"What you do now?" Tames Horses asked.

"Jim has my rifle, my hat, probably, and my Colt. He's with Alice Cantrell, I figure—and she's on her way to Spotted Pony's camp on the Powder River to find her brother. I'd like her to find him."

"Why?"

"Maybe she can talk him into going back East and leaving Spotted Pony's camp. The way I look at it, he's a bad influence."

"Then I go with you."

"Don't be crazy. The Blackfoot have long been enemies of the Nez Percé."

"Is not the famed and terrible Golden Hawk also an enemy of the Blackfoot?"

"I'm expecting Alice Cantrell to speak up for me. She must have some influence over her brother, and he sure as hell has some over Spotted Pony. That should be enough protection for me."

"And Golden Hawk will be enough for this old chief. He will come with you."

"Suit yourself, chief. And thanks."

"But if my arm falls off, I will have to stay here."

Hawk grinned at him in the darkness. "Just tell me when it starts to itch."

They made ready for bed and soon they rolled into their blankets, well back from their camp-fire's glowing embers, their mounts a good distance away on the other side of a ridge in a well-hidden draw. It was a precaution they were glad they had taken when, close to dawn, they heard the pad of moccasined feet on the trail below and slipped through the trees to investigate.

Through the moonless darkness they peered at a dim line of Bannock warriors padding silently along, heading south and away from the Blackfoot. Most of them were on foot and what ponies they had managed to escape with they were leading, in order to rest them.

But what caught Hawk's immediate and star-tled attention were the two captives trailing behind the last Bannock on long rawhide tethers looped over their necks. One was a woman with red hair, the other a powerful man with a notice-able hump on his back. Alice and Jim!

Hawk was about to snatch up his rifle when he heard the sound of unshod ponies in the timber behind him. At once he realized that under the present circumstances, any sudden, poorly thought out action would be foolhardy in the extreme.

All about them in the timber, fleeing Bannocks were as thick as flies in May.

Cautiously, he and Tames Horses turned and worked their way back through the inky night to their camp in time to see four intent Bannock warriors examining the still-warm embers of their campfire. Finished with their inspection, the Bannocks peered carefully about, then moved on.

As Hawk remained crouched beside Tames Horses, he realized that finding Spotted Pony's camp was no longer his main concern. First things first. And right now, the first thing to do was take back from the Bannocks their two white captives. It would not be an easy task. This aroused hive of fleeing Bannocks would not be an easy nest to penetrate.

But at least Hawk might be able to retrieve his rifle and Colt a hell of a lot sooner than he had expected.

—6—

As Hawk vanished over the falls, Alice Cantrell gasped, then slumped to the ground. Jed was dead. There could be no doubt of it. In that brief glimpse she had of him he had seemed so helpless—like a straw being swept along in a flooding street gutter.

She felt Buffalo Jim's comforting hand on her shoulder and told herself not to pull away. From the very beginning she had been appalled at his deformity, one he seemed to take so calmly, and had tried to dismiss it just as easily; she had no wish to hurt this big, patient man who had at times the simple, honest eyes of a child.

Fighting back the revulsion she felt, she peered up at him through hot tears. "Oh, Jim. What do we do now?"

"We go on. Find your brother."

"But you've been wounded. That arrow left a terrible gash in that . . . I mean, in your back."

He smiled, understanding everything. "In my hump, you mean. But that's the virtue of the damned thing. It takes all kind of punishment without a whimper."

Alice felt suddenly ashamed. The man's rueful modesty, his clear-eyed vision of who and what he was, humbled her.

"We better move on right away, Alice. This here ain't the healthiest piece of land for us. Not right now it ain't. We better get a move on, I'm thinkin'."

"Yes. Of course."

Wiping the tears from her eyes, Alice stood up and walked back with Jim to their horses. Mounting up, they rode north toward the Blackfoot lands—and Spotted Pony.

Four days later, riding across a clearing toward the sound of running water, they were surrounded by six mounted Bannock warriors.

Both pulled up, and in that instant Alice realized how much wiser had been Jed's plan to move through this Bannock country only at night. They were outnumbered and there was nowhere to run. Alice heard Jim mutter an obscenity. His sentiments mirrored hers exactly.

After riding around them in a tightening circle, the Bannocks flung themselves from their ponies and approached, their faces grim with purpose. The first Bannock to reach Alice grabbed her thigh and yanked her brutally from her saddle. She landed hard and on her back, but before her attacker could follow up his advantage, she managed to jump up and slap him in the face . . . hard. For an instant the Bannock stood before her, astounded. Then he stepped forward and punched her in the stomach, following through with ruthless precision. Alice plunged, retching, to the ground. A foot caught her on the side of

her head. The sky swung crazily across her field
of vision and after that she remembered nothing
more.

Someone was poking her in the back with a
sharpened stick. She opened her eyes and found
herself stretched out on the floor of an Indian
lodge, her cheek resting on the damp ground.
Her head throbbed dully from the blow that had
rendered her unconscious, but the discomfort
was bearable. She turned her head enough to see
the small Indian boy, his raisin-black eyes intent,
who had awakened her. When she tried to move
her arms to rise up and support herself, she
found that her hands were bound behind her,
the rawhide cutting cruelly into her wrists.

She heard Jim's muffled voice beside her. "Lay
still. Don't move. Don't let the devils know you're
awake."

At once she complied, allowing her cheek to
rest back down onto the tepee floor. There was
nothing she could do anyway, not with both hands
tied behind her. But she wished the boy would
leave off tormenting her. Squatting behind her,
he seemed as unmindful of the fact that he was
causing her pain as if he were poking an animal's
dead carcass.

An Indian woman entered the lodge and shooed
the boy out, untied Alice's wrists, and rolled her
over, not at all gently. She had a bowl in her
hand, but the aroma that came from it turned
Alice's stomach and she closed her eyes, remaining as limp as before. The woman slapped her.
Reluctantly Alice opened her eyes. The Bannock
woman thrust the bowl at her. Alice took it.

There was no spoon. She was expected to lap at the bowl's contents like an animal. The smell grew more vile the closer she drew it to her. She hesitated.

The Bannock woman, tired of this, flung herself upright and loosed a torrent of incomprehensible words at Alice. She obviously wanted Alice to take the food offered her and no nonsense about it. Alice glanced quickly at Buffalo Jim. Like her, he had been flung facedown on the tepee floor, his hands bound behind him.

"Better do what she says," he told her, his mouth barely moving.

"What is it? It smells horrible."

"Buffalo brains."

"My God!"

"It's an acquired taste."

"I can't anyway. I have to relieve myself. My bladder is fit to burst!"

"Tell the squaw. She'll understand that. And she sure as hell won't want you smellin' up her lodge."

Alice looked back up at the Bannock woman, put down the bowl, and pointed graphically to that portion of her anatomy in distress, her face eloquently expressing the discomfort she felt. The woman understood at once and dragged Alice to her feet and out of the lodge.

The bright, late-afternoon sun almost blinded her as the Bannock woman pulled her downstream. When those women washing clothes in the river's shallows saw Alice being yanked along and guessed the reason for it, there were catcalls and shrieks of laughter. Never in all her life had Alice felt this embarrassed—debased, really—and she was furious, not only at the Bannock woman leading her, but at herself for allowing all this to happen to her.

The Bannock woman pointed to a bed of rushes under a clump of willows lining the stream's bank. Face crimson, Alice hurried into the reeds, the water seeping over the tops of her boots as she loosened her belt. Having forsworn long skirts when traveling in this country, she regretted her decision now as she struggled to peel down her trousers. Her task completed, she squatted as low as she could get so as not to be observed by the grinning Bannock women lining the banks.

She was in that indelicate position when she heard screams from the Bannock women standing in the water. She turned her head and saw a band of yelping warriors galloping across the flat toward the village. Abandoning the clothes they were hammering a moment before, the women scrambled up the banks and, still screaming at the top of their lungs, raced for the village. The Bannock squaw who had dragged Alice from the lodge forgot her and dashed back to the village along with the rest, screaming out to her children in fear and panic.

It was this wild caterwauling more than anything else that alerted the Bannock braves, whom Alice saw snatching up their weapons and leaping onto their ponies. In a moment the Bannock warriors were streaming from the village to meet their attackers, their war cries enough to drown out those of the women urging them on. It was, Alice saw, a surprisingly small force of attacking Indians for a village this large, and she did not see that it had very much of a chance.

But that was unimportant. For the moment she was free. No one was paying the slightest attention to her. Staying in the water and keeping low, she moved along the embankment, following the stream back to the village. With little difficulty she located the tepee where she and Jim had been taken. Hauling herself up onto the embankment, she peered quickly about her. The attention of everyone in the village was focused, not on her or the stream behind her, but on the warriors racing out onto the flat to do battle.

She dashed to the lodge, lifted the flap, and ducked inside. Buffalo Jim was on the floor of the tepee, his hands still bound behind him. Snatching up a knife, she slashed through the rawhide. Jim sat up and began rubbing his hands to restore circulation, looking at her in some amazement as he did so.

"You got free and came back for me?"

"I couldn't just leave you."

"Well, I sure do appreciate it. How's the Blackfoot attack going?"

"You mean those are Blackfoot Indians attacking?"

"Sure. That's what the cry was that swept the village. A small Blackfoot force, I gather, charging the village in broad daylight."

"Yes, that's right. They don't seem to stand much of a chance."

"Don't lose any sleep over it. The important thing is, now maybe we can get out of here."

Retrieving Jed's rifle and Colt, his own knife and weapons, he handed Jed's rifle to her, telling her it wasn't loaded, but was heavy enough so that in a pinch she could use it as a club.

Alice got little comfort from that, but she followed Big Jim without a word as he led the way from the lodge to the stream. It did not appear to be too deep, but she was a good swimmer and more than willing to swim across if it came to that. This was not what Jim had in mind, though. Keeping close to the embankment, they splashed downstream, heading toward the distant pony herd.

"Can you ride without a saddle," Jim asked her.

"Yes."

"Without reins?"

"I can manage."

"If you can, you're some woman."

"To get free of that Bannock woman, I'd do anything."

"If you're interested, her name's Tree Woman. I heard her husband calling out to her when he grabbed his weapons and lit out."

"I don't care what she's called. I don't like her. Or that boy of hers."

Jim chuckled and kept going.

Glancing back at the flat where the battle was supposedly taking place, she could see Indians galloping after Indians and doing an awful lot of yelling and brandishing of weapons. It didn't look like anyone was getting hurt; it almost looked as if the attacking Blackfoot had changed their minds and were now running away from the more determined and certainly more numerous Bannock force.

"Maybe those Blackfoot would know about my brother," Alice called to Jim. "They could even be from Spotted Pony's band."

"I doubt it. Spotted Pony's band is way north of here—somewhere on the Powder. But it wouldn't do us any good if that was Spotted Pony's band," he continued, clambering up the steep cutbank to peer over the lip. "Looks like them Bannocks are closer to catching up to them Blackfoot. They'll cut that small force to pieces. Them Blackfoot can act mighty dumb at times."

Alice climbed up beside Jim and was in time to see a spectacular reversal of the Blackfoot's situation. Jim gasped, as surprised as she was, as a much larger force of Blackfoot suddenly erupted from the timbered slopes beyond the flat. Some of the Blackfoot headed directly for the unprotected village, while the others overtook the Bannock warriors from behind, falling upon them with sudden murderous effect.

His voice hushed, Jim said, "I spoke too soon, looks like. These here Bannocks are done for. I never did see the Blackfoot pull a stunt like that before."

"What do we do now?"

"Keep going to that pony herd and get the hell out of here," he said, pulling Alice after him.

The screaming that now came from the village caused Alice to glance back. A stream of old men and even a few young braves erupted from the village, herding women and children ahead of them. Like Buffalo Jim and Alice, they were heading downstream toward the pony herd.

By the time Alice and Jim were within a few hundred yards of the herd, the fleeing Bannocks had nearly caught up with them. For a moment Alice cringed away from them, terrified, but in their anxiety to get away from their attackers, the Bannocks overtaking them treated the two fleeing whites with the same indifference wild animals showed one another when fleeing a forest fire.

They reached the pony herd and were hurrying to catch a mount when abruptly, into the Bannocks' midst, a mounted Blackfoot warrior charged. Flinging himself from his pony, he began flailing away with his war club at a white-haired old Bannock. As Alice shrank back, she saw the old man, his skull shattered, fall to the ground. With an oath, Jim left Alice's side and hurled himself at the Blackfoot warrior. Startled, the Blackfoot warrior was too late to defend himself as Jim buried his huge knife into the Blackfoot's chest, plunging it in repeatedly.

Alice averted her eyes. The pure savagery of Jim's attack sickened her. Yet, at the same time, she felt an unholy joy at seeing the Blackfoot warrior struck down.

Sheathing his knife, Buffalo Jim came back for her and grabbed her arm. "Forget the ponies," he yelled, pulling her swiftly along with him. "All we can do now is make for cover."

"Where?"

"Across the flat. In that timber."

Gasping at the pace they were setting, Alice managed a brief glance back and saw mounted Blackfoot warriors pouring out of the village, heading toward the pony herd, while just behind Alice and Jim streamed more and more Bannocks heading, like them, across the flat for the security of the wooded slopes.

A moment later, out of breath and hardly able to stagger forward, they reached the timber, and not long after became part of a steady swarm of fleeing Bannocks, all of them too stunned, too broken by their defeat to pay Alice or Jim much heed.

At least for now.

Later, as Alice continued up through the timber, she glanced back down at the river valley. Funnels of black smoke were pumping steadily skyward from the spot where the village had been, and she imagined she could hear women screaming.

And then she realized it wasn't her imagination.

It was night. Alice was crouched beside Buffalo Jim, peering through the trees at a Bannock campfire. They had long since distanced themselves from most of the fleeing Bannocks, but Alice was bone-tired, her face scratched and raw from the countless branches that had whipped at it as she plunged along; she had endured it all without complaint. But that fire, its light glowing through the trees, had drawn her like a moth to a flame, reminding her and Jim how hungry and weary they were.

Bannock women were hunched about the fire, intent on cooking a late supper, it appeared. Despite the deprivations of that day, they were squealing out in some delight, and the level of their enthusiasm was climbing rapidly. What were they cooking? Alice wondered. Abruptly, a cold chill fell over as something deep inside her warned her to look away.

"Jim . . . ?" she whispered uncertainly. "What . . . what are those women doing?"

"You mean you don't know?"

Frowning, Alice looked more closely. One of the squaws had moved, giving Alice a clearer view of what was going on. Alice groaned inwardly, her stomach churning. They had a Blackfoot warrior at their mercy and were bent over him, cackling like witches around a caldron, smoking sticks in their hands, poking deliberately at the naked warrior, paying particular attention to the man's most vulnerable anatomy. Some had knives. Their laughter rising to a hideous shriek, they moved still closer, the better to practice their skills.

Alice looked away, appalled.

"Ain't pretty, is it?" Jim said. "They got themselves a Blackfoot all to themselves."

"But they're torturing him."

"That they are."

"How awful! Reading about such things is one thing. But actually seeing it ... It's so ugly, so bestial. At least he's not moving. Maybe he's already dead."

"Wouldn't count on it. Them Blackfoot buzzards can take a lot of punishment. It's a matter of pride with 'em." He shook his head grimly. "And then again, it's a matter of pride for them Bannock squaws not to kill a man right away. Spoils their fun."

Alice shuddered. "Let's get away from this."

"Suits me."

But they hadn't gone far when they were suddenly surrounded by two mounted Bannocks and a crowd of women.

One of the Bannock women was their former captor, Tree Woman. Shrieking, she pounced on Alice as if she were a chicken that had escaped just before plucking. Alice pulled angrily away, and when the Bannock woman again reached for her, Alice slapped her sharply. With a shriek, Tree Woman lunged for Alice, but as the Bannock men watched in admiration, Alice knocked her back. Then two other Bannock women joined the battle and proceeded to pummel her mercilessly until Alice sank to the ground under the weight of their combined onslaught.

Tree Woman reached down, grabbed a fistful of Alice's thick hair, and yanked her upright with brutal efficiency, once more binding her wrists with rawhide. On his feet beside her, his own hands already tied, Jim looked over at her.

"Ain't this where we came in?" he growled wearily.

"I'm afraid it is," Alice managed, unable to keep the bitterness out of her voice.

"Just don't lose hope. We'll get out of this."

"I'm beginning to wonder," Alice muttered as she felt Tree Woman drop a rawhide noose over her head.

Much to Alice's relief, they reached the other Bannock band a few hours before dusk of the next day. The Indians in this village, however, seemed little better off than Alice and Jim's captors. There were many women and children about, with a sprinkling of white-headed ancients, but few men and even fewer lodges.

Tree Woman untied Alice and Buffalo Jim, and before they could slump to the ground in pure exhaustion, she prodded and slapped them with a heavy willow switch while pointing to a spruce tree in front of a narrow ravine. Without argument, they made for the tree, while Tree Woman and her family headed for the ravine, the narrow interior of which was going to serve as their lodge, apparently.

Alice and Jim slumped to the ground under the spruce. Leaning her head back against the tree, Alice closed her eyes, grateful for this chance to get off her feet. But before long, despite her weariness, she found herself unable to ignore what was going on about her.

Bannock warriors and their wives and children kept riding into the camp, some of the men wounded terribly. Women on foot straggled in later, dragging young ones behind them or carrying babes on their backs, some in their arms. With each new arrival, it seemed, a deeper and deeper gloom descended over the encampment as women and old men—on hearing of the death of a loved one—began keening and wailing for their dead.

Alice was forced to look away as some women, in an excess of grief, sliced off their fingers with axes or slashed themselves in the breasts with hunting knives. One woman tore out great handfuls of hair in her frenzied grieving.

Buffalo Jim saw the look on her face.

"Pretty awful, ain't it?" he told her. "But these Bannock women don't really put their hearts in it. You should see how the Blackfoot women take on when their lord and master gets himself killed. It's a damn sight bloodier, and more often than not fatal."

"How awful."

"They's savages, that's the truth of it. But I

hear tell widow women in India throw themselves on their husband's funeral pyre."

"It's called suttee. Hindu women do it to prove their devotion to their dead husbands."

"So maybe this ain't all that strange."

"I find it strange, Jim—strange and sad. Very sad."

"Don't look then."

"I wish it were that easy." She frowned. "Jim ... over there, by that fire. Those women are at it again with that Blackfoot captive."

"Yep," he said. "Don't look like that poor son of a bitch is going to get much sleep tonight."

Alice looked pleadingly at Jim. "Isn't there anything you can do? You told me once ... I mean, you said the Indians were afraid of you."

"Because of my hump, you mean. That's right. They call me Buffalo Man and walk around me real respectful like."

"I didn't mean to mention it."

"That's all right. I knowed you was curious. Most people are. 'Course, they don't say nothin'. They just look. That's why I like kids. They come right out and ask you what happened."

"What *did* happen, Jim?"

"Fell off a wagon haulin' logs when I was a kid. One of the logs rolled over my back, broke my shoulder all up, the shoulder blade especially. There weren't no doctors to fix me up, so I just kept myself as quiet as I could until the pain stopped. When I could finally get up and move around some, I was all twisted up back there. Been that way ever since. But it looks worse than it is. I get around without no trouble— pretty good in fact."

"Yes, you do, Jim."

Jim was silent for a while, looking over at the Bannock women playing with their Blackfoot captive. Then, with a quiet sigh, he stirred himself and got to his feet. "Guess maybe I'll see what I can do."

Almost at once Alice was sorry she had asked Jim to meddle with those evil old women. They seemed like such terrifying harpies to her. But he was gone before she could call out.

Striding casually up to the campfire, Jim pushed aside two of the women. Then, reaching down, he flung the Blackfoot over his shoulder. Screaming hideously at him for taking their plaything, the women followed after him as he moved off. Jim just kept going, taking no more note of the woman than if they had been a cloud of gnats. As he neared the ravine, Tree Woman emerged from it, a switch in her hand, and began beating on Jim. He dumped the Blackfoot unceremoniously to the ground, snatched the switch from her, and tossed it away. Squealing in outrage, she brought two Bannock braves hurrying from the ravine.

Jim turned to face them. At sight of his massive, bearlike figure standing calmly before them, the two Bannock braves halted. Jim said nothing, just waited, allowing them to take a good look at his heft. Then his expression softened and he said something to one of the braves. A quiet conversation followed, the other brave joining in, after which the Bannocks waved away Tree Woman and the others. Jim picked up the Blackfoot and carried him to the other side of the spruce, where he let him down none too gently.

"Jim," Alice demanded, "what on earth did you tell those two Bannocks?"

"I told them I was Buffalo Man. I impressed upon them that my magic would enable them to hunt the herds next year with great success, that they would bring down only fat cows and no Blackfoot warriors would interfere with their hunt."

"How could you possibly make such a promise?"

"Who knows? Maybe next year they'll kill plenty of buffalo and the Blackfoot won't bother them, just like I said."

Alice looked over at the Blackfoot. Still unconscious, he was on his back, naked, his face bruised almost beyond recognition, his torso a mass of cruel wounds. Two digits on each hand had been cruelly amputated. Alice looked away, shuddering. "What can we do for him, Jim? He's in terrible shape."

"We already did what we could. We took him away from those damned harpies. We ain't in no position to press our luck."

Tree Woman approached with her husband. It was clear she was a bit more wary of Jim this time. Silently, the two Bannocks tied their hands behind them. Then, still without uttering a sound, they moved over to the Blackfoot and bound him hand and foot also.

Jim asked Tree Woman something. She laughed, then kicked him in the side and pointed to the trussed Blackfoot.

As she and her husband walked back to the ravine, Alice asked, "What was that all about?"

"I asked her for something to eat. She told me

we should eat the Blackfoot, we want him so much."

"Maybe we made a bad deal, Jim. I could eat a horse."

"Try not to think about it. Close your eyes and get some sleep. You'll need it."

She closed her eyes and tried to get herself comfortable against the tree. After a moment she felt Jim move closer to her and it seemed as natural as breathing for her to lean her head back against his chest. He smelled like a buffalo, she realized. But, then, so must she. But it didn't seem to make any difference to either of them.

For the first time in many days, she felt unaccountably content—and immediately fell asleep.

— 7 —

Hawk and Tames Horses peered down at the crowded camp, waiting for it to settle down for the night. Even though it was close to midnight, this threatened to take a while.

A steady stream of Bannock survivors had continued to straggle into the village throughout the evening, and with each new arrival a fresh outcry arose as old men began their lament and women their frenzied screeching and wailing. From the look of things, there was going to be a sharp increase in the number of women with scarred breasts and truncated fingers.

"How's your arm, chief?"

"Like you say, it get itchy. I want to take off splint."

"Keep it on a while longer. Can you work your fingers?"

"Not much."

"Stay up here, then. Keep the horses safe."

"I know what to do." Tames Horses peered more closely down at the village. "Buffalo Man and the redhaired one are asleep. Why is that Blackfoot with them?"

"Beats the shit out of me, chief."

For another hour they waited in silence. By then it appeared that the encampment was finally quieting down. Most of the fires were out and there hadn't been a new arrival for at least two hours. Hawk decided it was time. He took out his knife and started down the slope. Glancing back, he saw Tames Horses going back for the horses, which meant he would be waiting with them some distance away on the other side of a shallow stream they had already scouted. That evening, Tames Horses had increased their remuda from two mounts to six. The exhausted, grief-stricken Bannocks had not bothered to put a guard on their meager pony herd, and the old chief had taken his pick.

Once Hawk reached the meadow, he moved along the base of the cliff, keeping in the brush. He passed the entrance to a narrow ravine and kept on until he reached the spruce under which Alice and Jim were sleeping. A camp dog approached, fangs bared, a low growl coming from deep in his throat. Hawk waited. A dog sniffing at new arrivals was nothing new to this village, not this night, anyway. Hawk let the dog smell his bowie's blade. Satisfied, the dog turned and vanished into the night.

The dog's growling had awakened Buffalo Jim. He was sitting up as best he could with his hands tied behind his back, grinning at Hawk.

"Jesus Christ, Hawk! We thought you drowned on us."

"Well, I didn't. Roll over so I can cut you loose."

As Jim did so, Alice came awake, took one look

at Hawk's face leaning close in the night, and stifled a gasp. Hawk sliced through the rawhide binding Jim and nodded to her matter-of-factly.

"That's right, Alice," he told her softly. "I'm not dead. Now let me cut through this rawhide."

As soon as she was loose, Hawk peered closer at the Blackfoot lying facedown alongside them, then glanced questioningly at Jim.

"Who's your Blackfoot friend?"

"Don't know what he calls hisself. The women here been havin' a fine old time with him. Alice wanted me to put a stop to it."

"And you did?"

"For now, at least."

"Is he from that band that attacked the Bannocks?"

"Maybe. Say, how'd you know about that?"

"I'll explain later. Maybe we better take him with us. Might come in handy. You willin'?"

"Sure. But watch out. He might be a bit touchy."

"Wouldn't blame him if he was."

Hawk stepped over the two and leaned close to the Blackfoot. The Indian looked like he'd been dragged through a mile of straight razors, but he was breathing regularly enough. Employing his rudimentary Blackfoot, Hawk asked the Indian if he was awake and could hear him. The Blackfoot, facedown, turned his head and managed a nod. Swiftly, Hawk cut the rawhide binding his wrists and ankles.

Leaning close to the Blackfoot, he said, "Come with us. We seek the camp of Spotted Pony. You know where it is?"

"I will take you," said the Blackfoot.

"Good."

Jim and Alice were rubbing their limbs to get the circulation back in them. Hawk pointed to a distant pine on the far side of the encampment. "I won't be long. Meet me there. I'll take you to the horses."

"Where you goin', hoss?" Jim demanded.

"To fetch my Colt and the Hawken. Which lodge are they in?"

"This ravine right here. The Bannocks what took us captive are usin' it for their lodge. Your weapons and mine are in there. I'd like to go in there with you, Hawk."

"I'd rather you see to it that Alice gets over to that pine like I said. If you hear a shot or anything loud indicating I messed up, get her the hell out of here."

"Where's them horses you mentioned?"

"Keep going north to a small stream less than a mile from here. There's a meadow on the other side of it. An old Nez Percé Indian will be waiting there with them."

"I'd sure like to go in that ravine with you."

"I know you would. Now, get Alice and that torn-up Blackfoot out of here. I'll wait until you're at that pine before I make my move."

Jim argued no more and vanished into the night with Alice and the Blackfoot. Hawk gave them plenty of time, then slipped into the ravine, cutting his way through a tangle of wild grape vines. Crouching low, he moved slowly along until he caught sight of two figures rolled up in blankets at the base of a sheer wall of rock. Hawk moved on past them to make sure there were no others, then returned to look through their possessions.

There was not much. Like all the other Bannocks, they had been wiped out by that Blackfoot attack.

He found Buffalo Jim's Kentucky rifle and his knife with little difficulty, but his Hawken was nowhere in sight. And then he saw it. The barrel was sticking out of the blanket the Bannock warrior had wrapped about himself. Moving still closer, he saw the Colt hanging from a bush over the Bannock's head. In the ravine's darkness, it was not easy to discern, hanging there in the shadows. The Walker was resting in a fine leather holster attached to a leather belt. Hawk had never bothered with a holster for the big Colt, but he sure liked the looks of this one. It was Spanish made, finely tooled, one of this Bannock's most-prized possessions, Hawk had no doubt.

Reaching over the Bannock's head, Hawk lifted down the belt and holster very carefully and buckled the strap around his waist. It felt snug. He liked it. He took the Colt out and examined its load, then thrust the barrel under the chin of the sleeping Bannock and nudged. Hard. The Bannock's black eyes snapped open. When he saw Hawk looming over him, he started to cry out, but Hawk rammed the muzzle in deeper. The Bannock went rigid. With his free hand, Hawk reached under his blanket and pulled his rifle out.

He heard a movement behind him. Whirling, he saw the Bannock woman standing over him, an upraised knife in her hand. Hawk had no choice. Before she could bring the knife down, he brought the Hawken around in a vicious arc, slamming her on the side of the head. As she crumpled, Hawk turned toward the lunging Bannock. The Indian was too close for Hawk to club with the rifle, so he fired point-blank into his chest. The Bannock stopped as suddenly as if he had run into a door. Hawk holstered the Colt, snatched up Jim's rifle, and lugging his own Hawken as well, charged out of the ravine and clambered up the timbered slope.

By the time the aroused village had discovered where the shot had come from and found the two dead Indians, Hawk was high above the village, melting swiftly into the timber, heading north.

Hawk reached the meadow where Tames Horses was waiting only a few minutes after Jim and the others did. The moon had risen and was almost directly overhead, flooding the meadow with an eerily bright sheen.

When Alice saw Hawk splashing through the shallow stream toward them, she broke from the others and rushed to meet him. He caught her in his arms and a moment later Jim was alongside him as well, grinning like a possum as he thumped Hawk on the back, all of them talking at once as they related their adventures since that crazed Comanche knocked Hawk off the bluff.

When Hawk finally finished telling them of the Blackfoot attack on the Bannock village he had witnessed, Jim was dumbfounded.

"Why, damn it all, Hawk, you mean to say you was up there all that time? You watched the whole blamed thing?"

"That's what I said."

"And you saw James," Alice exclaimed.

"If that's who it was," Hawk admitted. "Though I don't see how it could have been anyone else."

"I don't either," she said, suddenly hushed. "He liked to talk about battle tactics. I remember that. It was all he found interesting at the Point."

"That, and gambling."

"Yes. That, and gambling. And now he's helping this Spotted Pony and his bloodthirsty band of Blackfoot Indians."

"That's what it looks like. And he sure isn't wasting much time. This isn't the first Bannock village he's attacked in the last week or so. He's keeping to quite a schedule."

"He's aimin' to wipe out the Bannocks, for sure," said Jim.

"And nearly causing his sister's death into the bargain," Hawk commented grimly.

"But, Jed, that's not fair. How could James possibly have guessed I would be a captive in that Bannock village? He can't be blamed for that."

Hawk shrugged and smiled at her. "All right, Alice. Maybe you're right. Anyway, that's all ancient history now. We're back on track if this Blackfoot can show us where Spotted Pony's camp is on the Powder. Have you spoken to him yet?"

"Not yet."

"Better go see him. I'd say he owes us."

As Buffalo Jim headed over to the Blackfoot, Hawk and Alice approached Tames Horses. The old chief's wrinkled face grew bright with pleasure as Hawk neared him. He had tried not to think of anything bad happening to Hawk in the Bannock camp and was glad to see him back safely.

"Thanks for your help, chief," Hawk told him. "Looks like we'll be heading out to Spotted Pony's

camp now. You can go on back to your people
and get that arm taken care of."

"You already take care of it."

"Yeah. Well, keep it clean, and when you get a
chance, tighten up them splints some, to keep
the bone straight."

"Why does Golden Hawk want me to go?"

"It's not that I want you to go chief. But it'll be
dangerous. Spotted Pony's camp, I mean."

"Does Golden Hawk prefer that Tames Horses
not go with him?"

"It's like I just said, chief. You'll be better off
not riding all the way to that Blackfoot camp.
You need to give that arm of yours a rest."

"Did Golden Hawk not mend Tames Horses'
arm?"

"Well, sure, I did my best, chief. But I can't be
sure it's— "

"Tames Horses is no more happy in the timber
alone. He find he is not so old, after all. He
would stay with Golden Hawk."

"You might get killed."

"Then I would not die alone—but with my
friend, Golden Hawk."

Hawk felt his throat tightening painfully.
"Come with us, then. By all means, chief. Your
wisdom and experience will help us greatly."

The old face brightened. "Tames Horses will
go now and fill his water jugs."

A moment later, as Hawk and Alice approached
Jim, the mountain man turned and hurried to
meet them. He looked very annoyed. "We got
trouble."

"What's wrong?"

"This Blackfoot won't have anything to do with

us—if we associate with a Nez Percé Indian, that is."

"You mean he won't guide us to Spotted Pony?"

"That's what the son of a bitch just told me."

Hawk brushed past Jim and headed for the Blackfoot, who was standing by one of the ponies Tames Horses had taken from the Bannocks. The Blackfoot had already fashioned a bridle out of a piece of rope Tames Horses had provided. As Hawk neared him, the Blackfoot vaulted onto the back of the pony and was about to wheel it around and gallop off. Hawk grabbed him about the waist, hauled him off the horse, and flung him to the ground.

The Blackfoot scrambled to his feet and rushed Hawk. He had no weapon, so Hawk did not draw his Colt. Instead, he sidestepped the Blackfoot, then brought the blade of his right hand down in a quick chopping motion. The rabbit punch caught the Indian on the side of his neck, slamming him into the ground like a sack of wet flour.

Hawk stood over him patiently, waiting for him to come around. When he did, Hawk hauled him upright. He winced when he got a look at the damage the Bannock woman had done to him, but that changed nothing. Hawk needed this Blackfoot if they were going to get Alice to her brother before the first snow fell. As he had told Jim, this Indian knew where Spotted Pony was camping along the Powder, and he owed them.

The Blackfoot shook his head to clear it, then fixed Hawk angrily with his smoldering black eyes.

"How are you called?" Hawk demanded in the Blackfoot tongue.

"Young Elk."

"Young Elk, in exchange for your freedom from the Bannock, you promised to take us to Spotted Pony's camp on the Powder River. Is the word of Young Elk worth nothing?

"This Blackfoot cannot stand the smell of the hated Nez Percé."

"If this white man can stand the stench of a Blackfoot, Young Elk can stand the smell of a Nez Percé."

"I am a Blackfoot warrior. I should take his scalp."

"Then will Golden Hawk take the scalp of an ungrateful Blackfoot! You would be turning on the Bannock women's spit now if it were not for Golden Hawk and his people. They have given you freedom so that you will ride once more with the great war chief, Spotted Pony. Is this your gratitude, then?"

The Blackfoot shook himself loose from Hawk's grasp and took an uncertain step back, his arrogance fading rapidly.

"Look over there," Hawk told him. "Do you know who that woman is?"

The Blackfoot glanced at her quickly, then shook his head.

"I will tell you who she is. She is the sister of the white man who rides at the side of Spotted Pony. Does he not also have red hair?"

The Blackfoot nodded, amazed.

"There is one more thing for Young Elk to consider. That old Nez Percé Indian was a great chief once. Now he is Golden Hawk's friend. Golden Hawk loves him as a father. Is this clear to Young Elk?"

The Blackfoot nodded sullenly.

"Now, what kind of a warrior is Young Elk?"

The young Blackfoot straightened his shoulders and did his best to meet Hawk's gaze squarely. "Young Elk is one who does not forget those who free him from the hated Bannocks. He is a Blackfoot warrior who keeps his promises"— he hesitated, as if he were struggling to swallow something loathesome—"even if he has to ride beside a stinking Nez Percé."

Hawk accepted this with a shrug. "And will Young Elk lead us to Spotted Pony?"

"Yes."

"How far is it from here?"

"It will take us four suns."

"Then we will waste no more time."

Four days later Hawk, scouting well ahead of the others, topped a rise just before dusk and found himself gazing down at the Powder River and, straddling both sides, Spotted Pony's village. Hawk was more than impressed; he was stunned.

He had never seen so many Blackfoot in one place at one time. It was obvious that more than one band now rode under Spotted Pony's banner.

Dismounting, he walked close to the edge of the rise and peered more closely at the Indian encampment. The first thing that caught his attention was the purposeful way in which the Indians were going about their business. The men were not riding aimlessly about or lounging in small groups, gambling. The women were busy, as usual, washing clothes in the river or walking briskly from place to place, while a great many more were busy scraping buffalo skins they had pegged out on the ground. What Hawk did not see were the usual gangs of near-naked Indian boys racing about chasing hoops or sticks. Also missing were the packs of snarling, ill-mannered dogs that usually roamed about any Indian encampment.

This was not a typical Blackfoot village. It was, more accurately, a solidly constructed, near-permanent outpost, replete with log buildings, barns, and sheds of all descriptions. Canvas-covered wagons were parked beside many of the buildings, and a corral alongside what appeared to be a large horse barn held more than ten draft horses. Surrounding these buildings were two neat rows of tepees, a formidable barrier obviously designed to protect these important storage warehouses, for that was what most of them resembled. There were many more Blackfoot lodges elsewhere, many hidden skillfully among the cottonwoods that lined both sides of the river.

With such a layout, Hawk realized, there was no way an attacking war party of Crow or Shoshoni could possibly surprise them completely or wipe them out in one single, devastating sweep—as the Blackfoot themselves had done to that Bannock village.

Farther down the broad river valley, the Blackfoot's swelling pony herd grazed peacefully under the watchful eyes of mounted Blackfoot pickets. Beyond the herd Hawk saw what appeared to be a huge field, its earth pounded bare from the constant punishment of unshod hooves. Hawk could barely make out ten or more small covered wagons lined up neatly below a small rise, and above them what appeared to be rudimentary breastworks. Hawk had seen similar drill fields in military outposts well down the Missouri.

Across the river, on a distant rise topped with spruce and pine, Hawk saw a long log house. It looked as if it had been only recently built—and to the specifications of someone used to living indoors.

Someone of importance from the East. A gentleman from West Point, most likely.

He heard the rest catching up to him, turned, and mounted up. Alice, anxious to reach Hawk first, was in the lead. He waited for her, and as she pulled up beside him, he pointed to the log house on the other side of the Powder River.

"See that?"

"Yes," she said expectantly, her face flushed in eagerness.

"Looks like that's where we'll find your brother."

"Thank God, Hawk!" Then she let her gaze sweep over the valley floor. "Why, it's like an army post, isn't it?"

"Except for all those Indian lodges."

Jim and Tames Horses reached them by this time, Jim halting on the other side of Alice, Tames Horses moving up alongside Hawk. Young Elk did not pull his pony to a halt, however. Instead, without a backward glance at his companions of the past four days, he rode on down the steep, grassy slope to the village below.

"Ungrateful bastard," muttered Jim.

Hawk had no intention of stopping Young Elk and was glad to see him go. Meanwhile, without comment, he let Alice and the others drink in the sight below them; it was apparent they were as impressed by what they saw as he had been.

"I wonder they haven't spotted us already," Jim told Hawk. "It sure don't look like they left much to chance."

Even as he spoke, four mounted Blackfoot warriors materialized from the timber, two on their right, a couple more coming up on their left. And Hawk did not have to turn around to know that more Blackfoot warriors were moving up on them from behind. Jim had spoken too soon. The Blackfoot had spotted them long before this.

As the Blackfoot surrounded them, Hawk noticed that all of them took special note of Alice—and especially her flaming red hair—almost as if they had been expecting her. Hawk leaned over and told Alice not to make a fuss. Her brother had sent an escort.

Still silent, and with an order close in precision to that of a military unit, the six Blackfoot warriors escorted Hawk and the others on down the slope toward Spotted Pony's village.

— 8 —

Following close behind the two Blackfoot warriors escorting them, Hawk took the ford across the shallow river and kept on up the far slope to the log building he had pointed out to Alice. As they neared the crest of the slope, Hawk got his first good, close-up look at James Cantrell.

Standing with his arms folded in front of his quarters, still wearing the wide-brimmed hat Hawk had noticed earlier, Cantrell cut a handsome, even dashing figure. The seams of his buckskin shirt and britches were elegantly decorated with quills and sewn-in glass beads. A heavy belt was buckled across his stomach and from it hung a flapped leather holster, the grips of a Dragoon Colt just visible. He was still wearing his saber, its metal scabbard burnished to a high gloss. He was as tall or taller than Hawk and as lean as a rake handle. His dark-red hair reached to his shoulders and the rakishly upswung tips of his mustache were oiled to a fine point. Soon Cantrell's lean, darkly tanned face became clearly visible, and Hawk felt Cantrell's burning eyes flicking from him to the others with a fanatical intensity.

Suddenly Alice spurred her mount through the encircling Blackfoot escort, and before they could stop her, she had raced up to her brother. Crying out to him, she flung herself off her horse and rushed to his side. Cantrell embraced her, the joy on his face unmistakable. There were tears on Alice's cheeks, and Hawk understood. For Alice this had been a long and dangerous journey, but she had reached her brother at last.

Looking away from his sister, Cantrell waved off the Blackfoot escort. The warriors wheeled and rode back down the slope. Hawk dismounted as Cantrell, with Alice by his side, walked toward them. Moving up alongside Hawk, Jim and Tames Horses also dismounted.

Alice accomplished the introductions. An Indian boy took their horses as Cantrell escorted them to his quarters. The log building had no flooring, but it contained a large living room with a fireplace, a kitchen, and two bedrooms. Cantrell led them into the living room and bid them make themselves comfortable. A Flathead Indian girl appeared in the kitchen doorway and Cantrell told her to bring them coffee.

The furniture was roughly but comfortably made from rude logs cut locally, and was covered by trade blankets and thick, soft furs. On the pounded dirt floor, a thick carpet of animal skins had been laid, with that of a huge grizzly in front of the fireplace.

Tames Horses sat cross-legged on the skin of a gray wolf, while Hawk and Jim made themselves comfortable in two large wooden armchairs. On a long, benchlike sofa across from them, Alice sat beside her brother. The Indian girl brought in their coffee on a wooden tray, serving them in large earthenware cups. Hawk took the coffee and sipped it. It had been sweetened with honey and was delicious.

"Now, then," said Cantrell as the Indian girl left them, "allow me, gentlemen, to thank you for escorting my sister through this wilderness."

"She's a very determined young lady," Hawk told Cantrell. "She would have come alone if Jim and I had let her."

"He's right, James," Alice admitted. "But I would not have made it without them."

Cantrell bowed graciously to the three men. "Again, you have my gratitude, gentlemen. You can imagine my amazement when scouts brought me word of a redhaired white woman proceeding toward this village. I had no idea Alice was even west of the Mississippi."

"James," Alice chided gently, "you must have known I would come after you."

"But why, Alice?"

"To take you back to civilization."

Cantrell sighed. "Yes, Alice. Indeed, I should have expected as much."

"And now we can go back, James. There's no need for you to hide out here."

"Alice," he reminded her gently, "I am not hiding—not hiding at all."

"But that's nonsense. Why else are you here? Surely you do not want to remain with these filthy, murderous savages."

Obviously embarrassed by his sister's unseemly vehemence, especially with a genuine Indian savage within earshot, Cantrell said, "Later, Alice. Later. This is no time to discuss such matters."

"Not too much later, I hope," she persisted. "There's no longer any reason for you to remain in this godforsaken land."

"It may be godforsaken in your eyes, Alice— but not in mine. At any rate, I am sure your escort is weary after their long journey and just might appreciate a chance to freshen up before supper."

"Sounds good to me," said Jim, getting quickly to his feet.

"Where we go now?" asked Tames Horses, getting up also. "I no sleep under wooden roof."

Standing up also, Cantrell laughed easily—a gracious host. "You can sleep anywhere you like, chief. But stay away from the Blackfoot village . . . until I can properly introduce you to Spotted Pony, that is."

"Where is Spotted Pony?" Hawk asked.

"Off recruiting more bands to join us. Gros Ventres. Bloods, Piegans. Northern Blackfoot."

"Seems to me you've got enough warriors already."

"Not yet. At least not for what I have in mind "

"And what might that be?"

"Later, Jed. Later," he promised, escorting the men to the door. "Tomorrow we will ride about and see the wonders I have accomplished with these savages. West Point discipline, it seems, goes a long way."

Before he stepped out the door with Cantrell, Hawk glanced back at Alice. After all she had gone through—the sight of Hawk apparently drowning, her long trek through wild, timbered country, her capture by the Bannocks—she had found her brother at last.

Only things were not turning out as she had expected. James Cantrell obviously lacked any real enthusiasm for the prospect of going back East with her. But Hawk knew Alice well enough by now to understand her dogged determination to accept no excuses. Her brother belonged back East, back in civilization with her, and she would not take no for an answer.

Hawk left the building with Jim and Tames Horses, Cantrell leading them back behind his house to a row of log houses set well back in among a line of pines. The quarters were newly built, and as Cantrell approached them, he explained to the three men—somewhat proudly— that these quarters would soon house members of his staff.

"Staff?" Jim inquired.

Cantrell halted. "Yes, Jim," Cantrell said proudly. "My staff. I've sent a man downriver to Independence to find the right men. Military men, I'm looking for, those with genuine battle experience—tough men, capable of leading these bloody savages and making them see the necessity for discipline."

"You plannin' on buildin' an army?"

"Precisely, Jim. Precisely. And tomorrow morning you will see how far I have come."

"I've already seen that," said Hawk. "I watched you and Spotted Pony attack that Bannock camp."

"I was in it at the time," Jim remarked ruefully. "So was Alice."

"Gentlemen, you must realize I had no idea she—and you, Jim—were in that village. How could I have possibly guessed such a thing? I thought of Alice as safely back East. Again, I must tell you how grateful I am that you managed to bring her safely to me through this wilderness."

Hawk shrugged. "Jim and I didn't want to see any harm come to her, Cantrell. She is a very determined young lady and loves you very much."

"Join me, Jed. You, Jim and your Nez Percé. I need men who know how to fight."

"Thanks for the offer," said Hawk, "but I have other plans. I can't speak for Tames Horses, though. Or Jim."

"Never mind," Cantrell said expansively. "There'll be time enough for such discussion later. You've had a long, hard journey. I'll have hot water brought for your baths and then we'll eat in a style and abundance you had thought far behind you. I've got hold of a shrewd Moddock trader who has opened a route for me south to the Comancheros. You'd be amazed at what goods can be purchased in Mexico, some items coming all the way from Spain."

"I can believe it," said Hawk as he continued on with Cantrell to the row of small log houses. He had an intimate knowledge of the Comancheros.

It was late. Hawk stood in the open doorway of his quarters. Behind him, Jim was snoring heavily. Somewhere out under the trees, Tames Horses had found himself a cool spot to sleep off the white man's liquor that had served only to fill the old warrior with melancholy.

The moon sat high in the night sky, so bright it banished the stars, shedding a powerful glowing luminance over the river valley below and Cantrell's headquarters. Cantrell had promised them a feast—and a feast it had been, sumptuous, amazing in its variety and abundance, with roast buffalo topping it off.

But Hawk was not thinking of the enormous quantities of food and drink he had just consumed. He was thinking of the Caesar of the New World, as Cantrell had styled himself. Though Cantrell should have been satisfied with what he had already accomplished, he was not. What he had now was only the beginning for him, like a faint whiff of catnip to an aroused cat. Toward the end of the feast, standing tall at the end of the long table, his glass raised in salute, his eyes flashing with a hectic, almost feverish glow, he had seemed almost mad. If not that, he was close to a kind of megalomania Hawk had heard about, what the ancient Greeks called hubris.

And Hawk wanted none of it.

Cantrell had extracted a promise from Hawk to accompany him the next morning on an inspection of what he termed his Mongol cavalry, and Hawk was bound by his promise to do so. But that done, Hawk planned to take leave of his host and this powerful Blackfoot outpost. Alice had reached her brother safely. With that accomplished, Hawk had other, more important imperatives to consider.

A great distance from where he stood now, in the midst of a high country sweet with the smell of pine and spruce—safe in the Crow village of her people—Raven Eyes was recovering from her fearful wounds, had probably already recovered. And Hawk wanted her. Every day that had passed since Hawk left her in her father's lodge, his longing for her had intensified and was now an intolerable ache.

He could remain away from her no longer.

He was about to go back inside and return to his bunk when he heard Alice calling his name. Looking over, he saw her emerge from the shadows surrounding her brother's headquarters. She was running toward him, her gown spectral in the moon's bright glow.

He left the doorway and went to meet her. Embracing him, she rested her head against his chest. She was trembling. "Take me," she whispered huskily. "I want you to take me! Please! You haven't drunk too much, have you?"

"Of course not. But what's this all about?"

She flung back from him, her eyes wild in the moonlight's glow. "What kind of a question is that, Jed? Don't you want me?"

"Hell, it's not that. But you coming at me like this, out of the night like a wild thing. I can't believe it's just me you want. Something's wrong. What is it?"

"There's nothing wrong. It's just that I want you. On the trail we couldn't do anything, not with poor Jim so close by, watching us. It would have hurt him too much."

Hawk had not been blind to Jim's deep affection—even love—for Alice, something that must have developed during his many days alone with her on the trail. "Then you realize how Jim feels about you?"

"Of course. A woman can always tell those things."

"And you feel nothing for him?"

"Please, Jed! I did not come out here to discuss Jim. You're all that matters to me."

She stepped quickly close to him and pressed her lips hungrily against his, her arms snaking about his neck, pulling his mouth down hard upon hers. He lifted his arms to grab her wrists and disengage her, but found himself encircling her neck instead, his own lips returning her wild, thrusting eagerness. It was not in him to refuse this woman's passion—not this night, even if she were lying in her teeth.

Lifting her in his arms, he carried her over to a level spot of ground in among the pines. Telling her to stay where she was, he went into his quarters for a blanket and a pillow. He returned with it, naked, and placed the blanket and pillow down beside her. She snaked onto it and flung aside her gown. The moonlight filtering through the branches bathed her pale body in a shimmering light and caused her pubic patch to gleam.

He fell upon her, rigid as a hickory stick, his lips encircling her nipples hungrily. Their two bodies were molten. He felt her twist and shudder beneath him, felt her arms tightening about his neck, her breath coming in short, jagged breaths. Then her pelvis lifted hungrily as her whole being yearned desperately for his penetration. Reaching under her buttocks with his hand, he lifted her off the blanket and thrust her under him, coming down hard, his erection sundering her. She gasped and flung her long thighs about his waist, scooting quickly, eagerly down, enabling Hawk to plunge still deeper into her.

Slowly, deliberately, he began stroking, savoring each thrust. Her arms tightened about his neck, pulling his lips down onto hers. They were alive, probing, teasing, wanton. Tiny sounds like those emitted by a small, terrified animal broke from her throat. Slowly, steadily, he accelerated his thrusts, increasing their depth, probing deeply into the sweet warmth of her, while her fiery fingers raked his back and her tongue darted like a snake's deep into his mouth.

He abandoned his controlled thrusting and let loose, allowing the intensity to build at a steady, remorseless pace. Thrashing about under him, she grunted like a wild animal. He felt his bowels churning into flame, the aching intensity building in his groin until he wanted to cry out—to howl.

And then he was over the edge, exploding into her with a wild, fierce abandon. At the same time she cried out, the muscles inside her tightening convulsively, her thighs holding him deep. She shuddered, grew rigid; flinging her head back, she let out a series of tiny cries as she climaxed. It seemed to go on forever as the hot, liquid warmth of her enveloped his vitals and he felt himself go rigid again.

Her lips reached up hungrily for his and she began to kiss him wildly, her tongue again thrusting like something alive. The arousal smell of her intensified. It was intoxicating, as was the sound of her fierce panting, the feel of her hot breath on his face. She was all woman now, lust unhitched from any traces, wild, unrestrained. Fully aroused once again, Hawk took charge, plunging deep within her once more, impaling her this time with a brutal, reckless abandon. He was part of her now, grafted to her flesh. Digging his knees into the ground for greater thrust, pleased at the sight of her tossing head, her wide eyes, the savage, unrestrained grunts of pleasure that broke involuntarily from her, he redoubled both the fury and the pace of his savage thrusting.

Alice climaxed before he did, moaning with the sheer ecstasy of it, writhing happily under him, while Hawk, heedless, continued to pound into her, until at last he came also—a long, shuddering release that caused his senses to spin. He chuckled softly and, feeling somewhat lightheaded, rolled off her. She smiled up at him and blew a damp lock of hair out of her eyes. They were both covered with tiny beads of perspiration, and the smell of their lovemaking was mixed with that of the pine needles and cedar thickets.

"Was that good?" she asked, her voice small, almost pleading.

"Yes. Very good."

"Am I a woman capable of satisfying a man?"

"Of course you are."

This was a conversation Hawk had never had before with a woman, and he wasn't sure he liked it.

"Am I as good as your Crow woman?" she demanded.

He felt himself go cold in his loins. "That's a fool question, Alice."

"Answer me!"

"I don't have to if I don't want to."

"You're afraid to admit it to me, aren't you? I'm as good or better than any woman you've ever had before."

"What the hell's the point of this, Alice?"

"I need you to do something for me."

"That's about what I figured."

"You don't understand. I want to marry you. I

am wealthy now. I told you about it. What I didn't tell you was the extent of my wealth. You will never have to work again. And neither will our children."

"You're taking a lot for granted, Alice."

"I have to. I have no choice."

He sat back and looked coldly down at her. "Tell me, Alice. What is it you want me to do for you—and for which you are willing to make me wealthy beyond my wildest dreams?"

"You are angry. Why are you so angry, Jed? Is my proposal so distasteful to you?"

"I'm waiting, Alice."

She sighed miserably. "It's James, Jed. You must help me. We must take him back East with us—away from this insanity."

"You just got here, Alice. What's the hurry?"

"Jed, he's gone mad. You should have heard him after you left. He imagines himself to be the leader of these aborigines. He's building an empire, he says. And he wants me to marry Spotted Pony. He says I can civilize Spotted Pony, teach him how to live under a roof and like it, be an example to the other chiefs."

So that was it. Alice needed him to save her from Spotted Pony—and save her brother from himself. And Alice had wanted this desperately enough to offer her body and then her hand in marriage. But now that he understood, he did not really blame her. If he had been in her shoes, he would probably have been just as frantic to get out.

"You know this Spotted Pony, do you?"

"I've never laid eyes on him."

"I heard he's a fine, upstanding Blackfoot chief.

He's sure smart enough, taking advice from your brother and then using it."

"Are you suggesting that I—"

"Why not? That way, you can keep an eye on your brother. Kidnapping your brother is an insane idea. You'd better forget it. Besides, you'll probably find Spotted Pony as good a man as I am."

She slapped him. He had expected it and took the slap without flinching. "I made love to you because I wanted a man. Is that so difficult for you to understand?"

"Nope."

"Then what's your complaint? You got back as much as you gave."

"And all I'm saying is you'll get back from Spotted Pony whatever you give him. If you're so all-fired anxious to look after your brother, stay here with him and take his advice. It just might work out."

"Are you siding with my brother?"

"I am not siding with anyone in this."

"Well, you'd better not side with James. Do you know what tribes he is going to attack next?"

"No."

"The Crow tribes along the Yellowstone. Didn't you say your Crow woman was from one of those bands?"

"I didn't, but she is."

"Then help me, Jed. James has got to stop this madness."

"Maybe so, but we won't stop anything by trying to kidnap him. He's a grown man, Alice, and he's going to do whatever he wants, no matter how unhappy it makes his sister or anyone else."

"Very well, then!"

She snatched up her nightgown and slipped it over her head. Then she got up and marched back to her brother's quarters. As he watched her go, he decided he had better find out how much of what Alice had told him was the truth. And tomorrow, during his tour with the self-proclaimed Caesar of the New World, would be as good a time as any.

The next morning, before they set out with Cantrell, Tames Horses removed his splint. Hawk inspected the chief's arm and was pleased to see how well his poultice had worked. Even where he had cauterized the infection, there was hardly any scar.

Hawk saw Alice watching the four of them ride out. Her brother waved to her, but she did not wave back. Hawk had said little to her during breakfast and she had made a valiant attempt to keep the conversation at the table light, but she wasn't fooling Hawk and she did not fool her brother.

As Hawk rode past the Blackfoot lodges, he was impressed by their clean appearance. Completely absent was the usual filthy clutter and the foul-smelling gutters that so often overtook Indian encampments when they became more or less permanent. As they were yesterday, the women were quietly busy washing or scraping skins they had pegged to the ground, while the screaming packs of children were still blessedly absent.

Again Hawk noticed how purposefully and alertly the braves moved about the village, showing little of the aimlessness he noticed so often in other Indian encampments, especially those close by trading posts. Instead of the usual circles of card-playing Indians sprawled on the grass, he saw active, intent groups busy repairing or cleaning weapons, making arrows or practicing their archery. Cantrell, it was obvious, had somehow managed to instill in Spotted Pony's Blackfoot band a surprising and genuine discipline—one that was clearly evident even apart from the battlefield.

Beyond the village, they passed the well-tended pony herd. It numbered at least a thousand head, the most obvious fruits of the Blackfoot's recent successes. They kept on to the flat Hawk had spotted the day before, the one resembling a drill field.

"Up here, gentlemen," Cantrell called, turning his horse onto a rise that gave an excellent view of the flat.

As Hawk pulled up beside Cantrell, he saw riding out onto the field neat columns of Blackfoot warriors. From the orderly, ramrod-straight manner in which they sat their mounts and the splendor of their war paint and weapons, Hawk realized at once that this display of fighting skill had been arranged by Cantrell especially for their benefit.

For the rest of that morning, Hawk and the others watched mounted bands of Blackfoot staging mock battles, overrunning emplacements or chasing down dismounted groups of "enemy" tribesmen. Intricate cavalry drills finished the display, with various mounted cadres—they appeared to be in multiples of ten—wheeled about, charging in first one direction then another, and all of it directed from a distant knoll by Blackfoot chiefs raising or lowering flags. When the sun rose high enough into the sky, a mirror was employed by these chiefs to signal a change of direction or reversal of tactics.

As the morning progressed, it was clear to Hawk at least that Cantrell was building himself a truly effective fighting force, and Hawk told Cantrell this without stint.

"Then you might join us?"

"I didn't say that."

"I tell you, Jed, we will sweep every tribe before us. It will change the course of history. How can you not want to be a part of this momentous undertaking?"

Hawk smiled. "Cantrell, there's a small Crow village I am anxious to visit—and soon. This, believe me, is all I want. I leave this empire to you, and to any like you who lust after such vast ambitions."

Cantrell shrugged. "Have it your way, then," he said, obviously disappointed.

They were about to start back to this quarters together when six Blackfoot chiefs crested a ridge close by and approached them. The chief leading them was a tall, broad-shouldered warrior in his prime with a bold chin, a sharp blade of a nose, and eyes that gleamed in pure defiance when he saw Hawk and instantly recognized him. Hawk knew at once that this was Spotted Pony.

As the chiefs pulled up a few yards from them, Cantrell greeted Spotted Pony and the other chiefs with him, then turned to Hawk and the others and told them to ride on back to his headquarters building, that he had business and would join them later.

Riding off, Hawk glanced back at Spotted Pony and the chiefs now gathering around Cantrell. Apparently, as a result of their recent victories, the Blackfoot chief had been able to recruit still more bands eager to fight under Cantrell's Blackfoot banner.

Cantrell arrived back at his headquarters later that afternoon. As he rode up, Hawk and the others stepped outside to greet him. Watching him dismount, Hawk noticed how pleased Cantrell looked. Evidently, his palaver with the Blackfoot chiefs had gone well. As Cantrell left his horse and started toward them, he smiled heartily.

"Got yourself some more allies, have you?" Jim commented. Hawk had already told him of Spotted Pony's mission.

Cantrell pulled up, pleased. "That's right, Jim. More tenacious Blackfoot warriors eager to ride with me and Spotted Pony."

"You told us last night you wanted to be the new Caesar, Cantrell, but why choose these Blackfoot to ride with? You're messin' with a tribe who don't take kindly to any white man—never have. They won't let a white trapper into their land. And I figure they must've killed a small army of trappers in the last ten years. What makes you so sure they won't turn on you?"

"They won't turn on me, Jim, because they need me. It's as simple as that. And as for why I chose the Blackfoot, why, you've answered your own question. It is just because they are such fierce and implacable warriors that I want them.

What I know about warfare will surely not be lost on such fighters."

"Any other reason?" Hawk asked.

"Yes, and you saw a demonstration of it this morning," Cantrell told Hawk. "The plains Indian is the greatest light-cavalryman in the world. With such a force Spotted Pony and I will be able to wipe these western plains clean. Soon enough I expect to open a trade route as far south as the Mexican border."

"There's some Comanches and more than a few Apaches might make that difficult," Hawk reminded him.

Cantrell smiled coldly. "They will be as easy to sweep aside as the Bannocks and the Crow—and every other tribe in our way."

"You talk pretty big for a newcomer out here," said Jim.

"Have you ever heard the saying that in the land of the blind, the one-eyed man is king?"

"No. Can't say as I have."

"Well, it's true. When it comes to military tactics, these Indians are blind. They have no discipline. Individual combat is all they understand or know. With them war is simply a game. They are afraid to sustain losses and peel off and flee whenever an enemy digs in and threatens to cut them down. Not only that, but for purely superstitious reasons, their war chiefs will sometimes cut a campaign short or leave with their men. More important, it is the fundamentals they neglect. They seldom if ever press home an attack or scout an enemy. And they almost never post pickets, leaving their villages and all their supplies vulnerable to sudden attack."

"And you'll change all that, will you?"

"With Spotted Pony's Blackfoot I already have. And the results are impressing every other warrior in the Blackfoot Confederacy. That is why so many of them are flocking to join me."

"But they are a hunting people as well as warriors," Jim reminded him. "How are they going to hunt if all they are doing is fighting?"

"Have you not heard of plunder? Tribute? Once we have attained mastery over these northern plains and the land south, we will take whatever we need from those settled regions adjoining us."

"Like Mexico."

"Yes, and Texas—and Missouri, if it comes to that," Cantrell admitted bluntly. "These savages will enjoy luxuries they could not have imagined. And meanwhile, of course, safe in their rear, their buffalo larder will remain intact, free from any plunder by other tribes. With their rich supply of buffalo robes and furs, their trade with the outside world will prosper as well. By that time, of course, they will be a nation among nations, secure in this great western land, invulnerable. No longer will their country be cut by white man's trails and invaded by predatory white men."

"By predatory white men, you include yourself, no doubt," retorted Jim.

Cantrell took no offense. "Of course," he admitted, laughing easily. "But I wager my predatory nature will be of more lasting value to these Blackfoot than your hunting and trapping of their mountains and streams. Unlike you wild fellows and others of your kind, I will leave something of infinite value behind when I pass on—a military tradition that will enable them to hold on to their land well into the next century and perhaps even longer."

"And as leader of this new nation," Hawk suggested, "you will be their first Caesar."

"Precisely."

Tames Horses had listened to all this intently, just as he had the night before. Hawk was not sure how much of it he understood, for he made no comment, content to lie back and study Cantrell closely with his shrewd black eyes. He was doing the same now. As for Jim, he finally shrugged and gave up on the discussion, evidently convinced there was nothing he could say that would shake Cantrell's almost maniacal certainty in his course of action. Cantrell had an answer for everything; it was all perfectly clear in his mind. He was going to save the Indians from the white man by turning them into a white man's army with himself at its head. And perhaps he was right, Hawk mused to himself. If the red man were to be saved, it might be the only way.

"Jed," Cantrell said, "let's take a walk. I'd like a word with you—in private."

From Cantrell's tone, Hawk sensed that something was amiss, and he found himself remembering the way Spotted Pony had stared at him earlier. As they headed toward the line of small cabins, Hawk caught a glimpse of Spotted Pony riding up to the headquarters building. The big Blackfoot chief did not bother to knock as he entered.

As they walked toward the line of small cabins where Hawk and his friends were now quartered, Cantrell came quickly to the point.

"You say you're Jed Thompson. Spotted Pony says you're Golden Hawk. Are you?"

"That's what some call me."

"Spotted Pony says you have long been an enemy of the Blackfoot. That you have taken many Blackfoot scalps. During that attack on the Bannock village, the one you say you witnessed, did you happen to run into any Blackfoot yourself?"

"I did. Two of them."

"Spotted Pony says you are the one who killed his brother and left his companion to die."

"Maybe I should have killed him, too."

"Spotted Pony has many brothers, but this was his youngest and was his favorite."

"What was I supposed to do—let him kill me?"

"I understand. And I am sure he does also. Spotted Pony also insists that you are a sorcerer, in league with the Great Cannibal Owl."

"I guess you know whether or not to believe that."

Cantrell's smile was a thin one. "Then you are not in league with the Great Cannibal Owl?"

"Afraid not."

They reached one of the empty cabins and paused by its open door. "This continuing enmity you seem to have with the Blackfoot, would you care to explain it?" Cantrell asked.

"Some years ago, after I escaped from the Comanches, I tracked my sister to a Blackfoot band. I had to go after her. I wasn't too careful how I got her back, just so I did. A few Blackfoot lost their scalps—or worse."

"And where is your sister now?"

"She's married and living in Cambridge."

"Massachusetts?"

"Yes."

He took a deep breath. "That is a very long way from here."

"It is."

"It is true, then. You have made many Blackfoot enemies."

"I guess you could say that."

"And now you have killed one of Spotted Pony's brothers."

"Looks like it."

"This is very difficult for me, Jed. Especially when I consider how much I owe you for bringing my sister safely through this wilderness. But I am afraid I promised Spotted Pony I would turn you over to him. Nothing personal, you understand. It is purely political. It will avenge him for the death of his brother and give him great renown among his people. And, I might add, it will enable us to attract still more warriors to our banner."

Before Hawk could say or do anything, Cantrell lifted the Colt from his holster and pressed the muzzle gently into Hawk's side. Then he smiled. "Don't try anything foolish, Jed. I could kill you now and make a present of your scalp to Spotted Pony. It would do much to cement our relationship."

Hawk was not wearing his Colt, but he had no intention of submitting quietly. His left hand flashing down, he grabbed the barrel of Cantrell's Colt and thrust it down, and then twisted Cantrell's wrist, forcing him to drop it. At the same time he swung on Cantrell, his fist catching the man flush on the jaw. With a startled gasp, Cantrell staggered back, his head striking smartly the open doorjamb. For an instant he hung there, dazed.

Aroused now to a quiet, lethal fury, Hawk punched Cantrell repeatedly in the face with a series of short, jabbing punches, driving him back into the small room. Under Hawk's furious pummeling, Cantrell went down with startling ease. Face slack, he struck the ground. Hawk took a step back.

That was when he smelled Indian.

He turned to see Spotted Pony lunging through the cabin doorway, an upraised war club in his hand. As the weapon swept down at him, Hawk flung up his arm to ward off the blow and twisted to one side. The stone club glanced off the side of his head, the blow enough to send Hawk reeling backward. The small of his back slammed into a table, which broke under his weight. He went down through it, crashing to the dirt floor, and found himself staring up at Spotted Pony as the Blackfoot chief flung aside his war club and unsheathed his knife.

Hawk reached back for his throwing knife. Spotted Pony struck down at him, his blade sinking into the dirt floor. Before he could withdraw it, Hawk plunged his own knife into Spotted Pony's back. The Indian was tough. With the knife handle protruding from his back, he spun on Hawk, whipping his hand around to catch Hawk on the side of his head. Reeling back from the blow, Hawk saw Spotted Pony scramble upright and lunge toward him a second time, his huge knife gleaming in the dim cabin.

Scrambling across the floor, Hawk snatched up Spotted Pony's discarded war club and lashed out with it, catching the already weak Indian on the side of his head. Spotted Pony grunted and tried to steady himself. On his feet now, Hawk swung the club a second time and stove in the side of Spotted Pony's skull. Incredibly, with his skull shattered, Spotted Pony kept on his feet, staring with some amazement at Hawk. Then he sagged onto the floor, his eyes cold-dead in his sockets.

Hawk glanced over at Cantrell and saw him pushing himself off the floor dazedly, his wide, incredulous gaze fastened on the dead Blackfoot chief.

"My God, Jed," he gasped. "What've you done?"

"I've killed Spotted Pony, Cantrell. Before he could kill me. You better pack your things."

"What . . . what do you mean?"

"It's your sister's idea."

"What?"

"You're reign is over, Caesar. We're taking you back."

—9—

At that moment Jim and Tames Horses burst into the cabin.

"We got trouble, Hawk," Jim cried. "There's a bunch of Blackfoot charging up the slope."

"Many wear war paint," muttered Tames Horses unhappily.

And then both of them saw Spotted Pony's form sprawled on the dirt floor, a dark puddle of blood spreading under his shattered skull. Dismayed, Jim turned quickly and glanced back out the open door.

"Looks like we got trouble," Hawk said, turning to the still-dazed Cantrell. "Maybe you better help me quiet those Blackfoot."

"You'll trust me to do that?"

"I don't have to trust you," said Hawk, stepping quickly out through the doorway.

He picked up the Colt Cantrell had dropped. Checking the load, he cocked it and stepped back into the cabin. Thrusting the barrel into Cantrell's back, he told him to move out and head off the Blackfoot.

"I don't think I'll do that," Cantrell replied.

Hawk simply pressed the barrel deeper into the small of Cantrell's back. "If those Blackfoot find Spotted Pony dead in here, it won't be just your scalp, it'll be your sister's as well."

Cantrell's view of the situation changed instantly. He moved over and stepped out through the doorway just as ten mounted Blackfoot warriors crested the ridge and galloped toward them. As Tames Horses had noted, they were all in battle dress, black and white war paint slashed across their foreheads and down their cheeks. At sight of Hawk and Cantrell, the warriors turned their horses in their direction.

Cantrell stepped quickly away from the cabin and went to meet them, Hawk staying close beside him, the revolver in his hand still boring a hole in Cantrell's back. When the Blackfoot got close enough, Cantrell held up his hand and called a greeting to the warrior leading them, addressing him as Red Feather.

The Blackfoot warriors yanked their mounts to a halt. Glaring down at Cantrell, Red Feather demanded, "Why is the hated Golden Hawk standing with you this day? He is an enemy of the Blackfoot."

"I will visit your camp tonight with Spotted Pony. Then we will speak of this business."

"Give us Golden Hawk now."

"No! Golden Hawk is our enemy, yes. But he has taken many Bannock scalps and has brought my sister to me. Now he has promised to use his magic to increase our power. But all this we will discuss in tonight's council. I speak for Spotted Pony. He wants you to return to the village and make ready for this night's council. Send a crier to inform the other chiefs. We will need their wisdom to settle this matter."

"I would hear this from Spotted Pony," the Blackfoot told Cantrell, his voice heavy with arrogance. "Red Feather does not think he needs Golden Hawk's magic." He looked venomously at Hawk. "It is of no more value than the piss of a rabbit."

"Do as I say," snapped Cantrell. "Spotted Pony will speak to the council tonight. Then we will settle this."

Red Feather's fury was almost palpable. He did not have to accept Cantrell's authority and he could have demanded that Spotted Pony himself step forward to corroborate Cantrell's statement. For a moment it looked as if Hawk might be forced to make his stand out here and he got ready to pull the revolver out of Cantrell's back to use on Red Feather and the other Blackfoot warriors. There was no way he and Cantrell would escape with their lives, but he would take many Blackfoot with him.

Abruptly, Red Feather shouted an order to his companions, wheeled his pony, and led them back down the slope toward the village.

Cantrell turned, his shoulders slumped, and looked bleakly at Hawk. "That too was Spotted Pony's brother. He is almost as famous a warrior as was his brother. But he has never accepted my authority and has fought me all the way. Now, with Spotted Pony's death, there is nothing to stop him."

Hawk saw Alice then. She was running toward them from the headquarters building, her cheeks glistening with tears. When she got closer, Hawk saw that her right cheek was swollen and purplish, as if she'd been struck with brutal force.

"What is it, Alice?" Cantrell asked, rushing to meet her.

"Spotted Pony," she cried. "The man you chose for me. When I refused him just now, he took me against my will."

"My God, Alice," Cantrell groaned, holding her close and stroking her hair to calm her. "I swear. It was not supposed to be like that."

"Well, it was!"

Cantrell glanced miserably back at Hawk. "Get your horses and provisions. You don't have much time."

"You're coming too."

"No. Someone has to stall Red Feather. That'll be my job. Just get yourselves and Alice out of here."

"You're going to try to salvage your empire?"

"Do you blame me?"

Two days later, before noon, Tames Horses overtook them and pulled alongside Hawk. "The Blackfoot come hard," he told Hawk.

"Who is leading them?"

"Red Feather."

"Was Cantrell with them?"

"I did not see him."

Hawk glanced at Alice. She was riding abreast of him, Buffalo Jim on the other side of her. Her still-swollen face had gone pale at the old chief's words, but she kept her gaze straight ahead and made no comment. Like him, she had expected—and was now forced to accept—the worst.

Hawk looked back at the chief. "How many are there?"

"Many."

"How long will it take for them to overtake us?"

He glanced at the sky. "Before dark maybe."

They were in high country. Ahead of them beckoned the entrance to a steep-sided canyon, its entrance obscured by timber. Hawk headed for it, and a half-hour later they rode into it. The steep slopes were thick with pine and juniper. This late in the summer, the broad, meandering stream that wound through the canyon was in places only fetlock-deep as it ran, clear as glass, over the streambed's sand and gravel.

They rode on into the canyon, single-file, keeping to the bed of the stream. Two miles farther on—forced to flow between a narrow defile—the stream's flow quickened and the water became deep enough to brush the belly of Hawk's mount as the pony bent its head and kept going against the current.

Once through the defile, Hawk saw ahead of them a quarter-mile or so of shallow rapids that vanished at the spot where the canyon turned, revealing the stark white face of a canyon wall so sheer only a few scrub pine had managed to find a toehold on its flanks. Beyond the rapids, the stream vanished behind a wooded neck of land. Hawk looked about him and saw off to his right a flat neck of caprock that shouldered out of the stream and lost itself in the willows crowding the shoreline.

He pulled up.

The rest did as well. As they turned to face him, he said, "I'm staying here. This is as good a spot as any to take on Red Feather. The rest of you keep going. Stay in this stream as long as you can before leaving the canyon, in case any Blackfoot manage to get by me."

"You mean us," said Jim. "I am staying with you, Hawk. Tames Horses can take Alice the rest of the way."

"No," said Tames Horses. "It is I who will stay with Golden Hawk. Buffalo Man go with redhaired woman."

Hawk looked at the old chief and knew there was no sense in arguing with him. He glanced over at Jim. "You heard the chief. Take Alice to Fort Hall. We'll hold the Blackfoot long enough for you to make it if you keep going through the night. Just don't look back."

Jim knew enough not to argue. Alice turned her horse and splashed closer to Hawk. Leaning out of her saddle, she wrapped her arms around his neck and pulled him close. He could feel her warm tears on his cheek.

"I am a wicked, wicked woman," she whispered in his ears. "Please, forgive me."

"No time for that now," he chided her gently. "Later. At Fort Hall."

She kissed him then, full on the lips. He returned her kiss, then pushed her back onto her saddle and looked over at Jim.

"Get out of here, Jim. And good luck."

Jim nodded curtly, turned his horse, and led Alice on up the stream, moving as fast as they could in the shallow rapids.

Hawk sat his horse and waited until they were nearly out of sight beyond the finger of land before guiding his pony along the caprock to the willows. Once in the willows, he and Tames

Horses kept in the shallows for close to half a mile before following a patch of gravel out of the water and into the timber.

Pulling up on the crest of the canyon wall not much later, they made camp, intending to give each other a half-hour of sleep at least before the Blackfoot arrived. For a moment Hawk gazed down at the canyon floor, satisfied they had found the best spot possible to spring their surprise on Red Feather.

They had already settled roughly on a course of action, one they could easily alter if events dictated. With Hawk's big Walker Colt, Tames Horses would discourage those riding through the narrow neck farther down, while Hawk, taking cover on the canyon rim, would range widely, using his Hawken to pick out any Blackfoot warriors that managed to make it through safely.

Hawk and Tames Horses could not possibly stop all of them, of course, not even a very great many—but they would sure as hell slow them down, maybe force them to pull back and make camp. Then, when night fell, Hawk would do what he could to see to Red Feather personally.

Maybe he would get to show him a bit of old-fashioned sorcery.

The Blackfoot ducked low on his horse and lashed it toward the rapids. Hawk aimed carefully and squeezed off a shot. The Indian peeled off his pony and was immediately caught up in the current. Tames Horses, crouched in the willows, had started it all a few seconds before with two quick shots that brought down two other Blackfoot as they charged through the defile. Now, three riderless ponies were trotting through the water toward the opposite shore. But more Blackfoot warriors were pouring through. Hawk kept up a steady, murderous fire from the canyon rim, not sparing his powder charges, ramming home each round thoroughly.

Meanwhile, Hawk could see beyond the defile at the milling swarm of mounted Blackfoot, all of them wildly upset at this sudden, unexpected attack. They could not have any idea how many armed men comprised the ambush, but Red Feather was urging his warriors on through the defile, nevertheless. But Hawk glimpsed other, smaller groups led by other chiefs and saw the chiefs holding their men back, some even retreating to the shore behind the main force. How quickly, Hawk realized, had Cantrell's influence in tactics been erased. Those Blackfoot warriors were supposedly under Red Feather's command, but they were as chaotically individual as ever, as if Cantrell had never existed.

After six more Blackfoot lost their lives or their ponies, no more riders charged through. Hawk waited awhile to make sure the Indians had given up their foolhardy effort to squeeze through, then moved on down the canyon's rim where, a few moments later, Tames Horses caught up to him.

"They leave their ponies now and come this way," he told Hawk, his eyes gleaming at the amount of punishment they had just inflicted on the hated Blackfoot.

Hawk nodded. It was what he had expected. The trail along this rim was the only other way the Blackfoot could proceed up the canyon, which meant that, before long, the Blackfoot would reach the rim and begin pouring toward them.

Hawk led Tames Horses into the timber lining the rim.

Both men led their ponies without bothering to hide their tracks. Once they were deep enough into the timber, they mounted up and rode a good distance along a trail they had tested out earlier. Then, leaving this trail, they led their mounts over rocky ground, tethering them at last in a narrow, wooded ravine, after which they trotted back to the canyon.

It was close to dusk when they heard the Blackfoot ahead of them, moving back out of the timber. Unwilling to follow the trail left by Hawk and Tames Horses in darkness, they were returning to the canyon rim, as Hawk had known they would, to make camp and lick their wounds. Hawk and the chief crept to the edge of the timber and peered out at the several campfires the Blackfoot had built.

"There is Red Feather," Tames Horses said, indicating a tall Blackfoot walking between two fires.

Hawk peered closely at the Blackfoot chief. He was with two other chiefs, the three talking with some animation. Hawk wondered if the two were not trying to convince Red Feather to give up this fool pursuit, that already they had lost more Blackfoot than they had when they attacked the Bannock villages.

Or perhaps they were urging him to continue on so as to properly avenge the death of Spotted Pony.

Hawk watched Red Feather break away from

the two chiefs and drop a blanket over his sholders as he settled by one of the largest campfires. As the two chiefs moved off, Red Feather took out his pipe. In a moment his head was enshrouded in heavy clouds of smoke.

Red Feather was coming to a decision . . . or trying to.

Hawk and Tames Horses melted back into the timber.

By midnight, all was ready.

Hawk's hoarse cry—the scream of the Great Cannibal Owl—echoed suddenly and harshly over the canyon rim. Braves sprang from blankets. Fires were suddenly fed and almost instantly blazed up to push back the darkness. Hawk stepped out of the timber and, facing Red Feather's camp, let out a second awesome screech.

There was no mistaking Red Feather's tall figure as he left his camp and took a few steps toward Hawk.

"It is me, Red Feather."

"I do not fear you, Golden Hawk."

"Then come after me. Alone."

"You are not alone. There is another with you."

"Then do not come alone."

Red Feather hesitated. He seemed to be peering into the timber, looking for someone. "Is the redheaded woman with you?"

"Why do you want to know?"

"Red Feather would have this woman for himself. In exchange, he will let her brother live."

"Cantrell is with you now?"

"Red Feather has not yet killed him."

"The redheaded woman has returned to the East. Red Feather will never see her again."

This news caused Red Feather to pause. His voice no longer so certain, he said, "Then go after her. Tell her if she returns with you, this new chief of the Blackfoot will let her brother live."

"You mean you will allow Golden Hawk to leave now so that he may go after the sister of this white man? You will not try to stop him?"

"Red Feather will not stop Golden Hawk."

In that instant Hawk knew that, despite his earlier bluster, Red Feather feared Hawk's reputation for sorcery. His willingness to allow Hawk to move off, ostensibly to bring Alice back to him in exchange for her brother's life, was only a thinly disguised effort to delay an immediate confrontation with Hawk. It remained only for Hawk to call his bluff.

"Is Red Feather an old woman who trembles in her lodge at the sound of thunder?" Hawk taunted. "What is this talk of sending Golden Hawk after the redheaded woman? It is Golden Hawk who killed two brothers of Red Feather. Is this how Red Feather avenges the death of the great Blackfoot chief, Spotted Pony?"

This scathing challenge, spoken in as eloquent a Blackfoot as Hawk could manage, carried far across the rim for every warrior to hear. Hawk thought he could see Red Feather visibly tremble in outrage.

"Red Feather will come for you," he cried. "And before your eyes he will take off the head of the redheaded woman's brother."

Red Feather turned and gave an order to a brave standing behind him. A moment later a pathetic, disheveled James Cantrell was pushed forward to stand unsteadily beside the Blackfoot chief.

Hidden behind Hawk in the brush to keep an eye on his flank, Tames Horses gasped in astonishment. Hawk himself was dismayed at what he saw. His face swollen and scarred with burns, his once luxuriant hair apparently ripped out by the roots, able to stand only crookedly because of the damage done to his right foot, James Cantrell was now but a pitifully torn-up remnant of the arrogant leader who had strutted before them such a short time before. He was Caesar no longer.

Pushing the beaten Cantrell ahead of him, Red Feather started toward Hawk. Hawk ducked back into cover and, with Tames Horses by his side, followed a previously prepared path that took them deep into the timber. It was an easy trail for Red Feather to follow, since Hawk and Tames Horses had been at some pains to make it so. Meanwhile, Hawk was under no illusions. He knew that once Red Feather vanished into the timber, the rest of his warriors would sift into the woodland after him, eager to back his play. Indians were superstitious and certainly foolhardy enough when taunted into action. But they were also realists, unwilling to see a capable leader lost if it could be avoided.

Reaching the base of a tall pine they had selected earlier, Hawk helped Tames Horses up into it, then watched with some apprehension as the old chief clambered up onto an overhanging branch on which the terrible and fabled Great Cannibal Owl now crouched, waiting. Hawk took cover beside the tree in a heavy screen of pine branches he had cut for this purpose. As he waited for Red Feather's appearance, he swiftly calculated his next moves. His original intent—to kill Red Feather and therefore demoralize completely his followers—was no longer his primary intent.

He had gone after Alice to help her find her brother. He, along with his two comrades, had succeeded in doing just that. But as Hawk saw it now, his job was not yet over. It was essential that he deliver James Cantrell from his captors and take him to Alice before she left Fort Hall for the journey back East. Hawk wanted Cantrell to live. Not only would he have a tale to tell, he would hereafter be a much wiser man—perhaps even a humble one.

The high moon cast a spectral glow over the trail Hawk had followed to the pine, and out of it came Red Feather and James Cantrell. Hawk thought he could hear the sounds of other Blackfoot warriors moving toward them through the timber. He stepped out in front of the pine and held up his hand to halt Red Feather. The Blackfoot chief stopped, Cantrell shambling to a halt beside him. Cantrell appeared dazed, as if he were moving in a dream, or more accurately, a nightmare.

"I am waiting, Red Feather," Hawk told him, displaying his long bowie knife, the blade gleaming in the moonlight. "Take me if you can."

"Where is the other one?"

"He has left you to me. I do not need the help of an old man to take the hair of Red Feather."

Uncertain though he was, Red Feather did not delay any further—and did precisely what Hawk had expected him to do. Grabbing Cantrell to use as a shield, he pulled his own knife and rushed Hawk.

For a moment Hawk made a pretense of holding his ground, then ducked back into the brush screen he had constructed. At the same time, from above them came the terrible screech of the Great Cannibal Owl as it swooped down out of the night. Huge, its enormous wings opening wide, the terrifying bird—known to feed on the flesh of all living creatures it found abroad at night—slashed at Red Feather, its talons digging cruelly into the flesh about the chief's head and shoulders.

Screaming in dismay and sheer terror, Red Feather slashed back wildly at the horror that had him in its grasp, and as he did so, Hawk stepped from the brush and with the barrel of his Colt clubbed the chief into insensibility. A second later the equally dazed Cantrell received a blow just as decisive and collapsed to the ground beside his captor.

At that moment Hawk could have killed Red Feather with one single, easily administered slash of his knife. But he did not. The Great Cannibal Owl was not supposed to own bowie knives, and Hawk wanted to leave no doubt in any Blackfoot's mind what it was that had reduced their chief to a quivering pulp.

Lifting off Red Feather the winged creature he had fashioned of woven pine branches, Hawk signaled to Tames Horses to haul it back up. Then, with the sharp, broken ends of branches he had already gathered, Hawk scoured out deep and terrible claw-like gashes in the unconscious Blackfoot's shoulders and thighs, not forgetting the upturned side of his face. Then he flung the still-unconscious Cantrell over his shoulder, and grabbing the rawhide rope Tames Horses had already lowered to him, he pulled himself swiftly into the pine.

Once they were high enough, the two men swung to a second, then a third tree, using rawhide lines already tied in place for this purpose. There, crouched high in the pine's branches, they watched the Blackfoot warriors pour through the timber toward their downed chief, his cries of a moment before drawing them swiftly toward the pine under which he lay. As they bent over him, Hawk saw the chief regain consciousness and cry out as for a horrifying moment he relived his awful encounter with the Great Cannibal Owl.

At once the other Blackfoot warriors, infected by their chief's abject terror, fled back with him through the timber toward the canyon rim, and soon the moon's spectral glow filtering through the dim columns of pine revealed a timberland empty of Blackfoot, while the only sound was the murmur of the wind in the pines' topmost branches.

Cautiously, after a decent interval, Hawk and Tames Horses climbed down and, with the insensible Cantrell slung over Hawk's shoulder, moved off through the timber until they reached the ravine where their mounts waited. Slinging Cantrell's still-unconscious body over the neck of Hawk's mount, they rode steadily south until well into the next day, when they stopped to take a needed breather—and to explain to a dazed and thoroughly astonished James Cantrell what had really happened back there in the timber.

—— 10 ——

It was time to say good-bye. Alice moved closer
to Hawk and embraced him, then kissed him
lightly on the lips. There was in the kiss only a
distant echo of the passion both had spent on the
other. Minerva Cantrell was on her way back to
civilization with her brother and was leaving
that other person, Alice Cantrell, behind in the
wild land she had journeyed through with Golden
Hawk.

"Good-bye, Jed," she said. "James and I will
think of you often." Then she turned to Buffalo
Jim and Tames Horses.

She embraced Jim warmly and nodded solemnly to Tames Horses. The old chief returned
her nod with a bemused nod of his own. She
turned away and then climbed up onto the wagon's seat and took the reins her brother handed
to her.

Then it was James Cantrell's turn. He looked
considerably better than he had when Hawk and
Tames Horses took him from Red Feather, the
man having pulled himself together with considerable courage and tenacity during his trip south

to the fort. And this past day and a half with his sister had done wonders for his morale. But he was no longer the swaggering Man of Empire he had been at Powder River, nor was it likely he would ever be again. To his credit, in the days since his return he had revealed an engaging sense of humor about his adventures, managing to cast the entire escapade in rueful perspective.

Hawk had been right. As a result of his awful comeuppance, James Cantrell had become a different—and a better—man.

Limping slightly, he stepped closer to Hawk. "I've told you before, Jed, and I'll tell it to you one more time. I'll never forget you three and what you did for us. If you ever make it back East—any one of you—you know for sure you've got a home with us."

"That's right neighborly," admitted Hawk, "and if I ever get tired of these mountains, I might take you up on that."

"Me, too," said Jim.

Cantrell looked at both of them and broke into a grin. "I can see in your eyes just how likely that will be. Well, anyway, I meant every word of it."

"Maybe for a visit," Jim said.

Cantrell shook Hawk's hand, then Jim's. Aware of Tames Horses' aversion to the white man's mania for handshaking, he contented himself with simply nodding his thanks as had his sister; then, still favoring his game leg, he swung up onto the seat beside her.

They were not traveling back alone. A teamster hauling a load of furs and buffalo hides had pulled out not long before and would see to it that they reached the Missouri without mishap. From there, Independence was only a matter of time and Hawk had no doubt that—after all they had been through—they would reach it safely.

"Good-bye," Hawk called, stepping back from the wagon.

The others joined in bidding them good-bye. Cantrell slapped the reins and the horses started up. MacPherson moved up behind Hawk then to add his good-bye wave to the others, and a moment later the wagon had vanished through the fort's gate.

"Now what?" said MacPherson, turning to Hawk, a mischievous gleam in his eye. "I'm afraid I don't have any more crazy white women for you to save."

"That suits me fine," Hawk replied. "I'm heading back to my cabin before the snow flies. I'm hoping I'll find Raven Eyes there ahead of me."

"I hope so too," Jim said.

"And what about you and Tames Horses?" Hawk asked Jim. "Where you bound?"

Jim grinned. "The chief here has promised to show me a valley fed by a stream choked solid with beaver, and in the timber, herds of elk and mule deer as tame as kittens. Maybe even a few stray buffalo."

"Sounds like the famous land of milk and honey."

"You come too," said Tames Horses. "Bring your woman. I don't mind Crow women. They are fine cooks."

"Maybe, chief. Right now, I'm a mite anxious about her. So I'll be pulling out first thing in the morning."

"Maybe we'll stop by on our way," Jim suggested.
"I'd like that. I'm sure Raven Eyes would too."

Weasel Piss had found a spot high on a ridge
that gave him an unobstructed view for miles
in every direction, especially the trail leading
through the timbered foothills between Hawk's
cabin and Fort Hall. Each day he sat cross-legged
on a grass mat he had woven himself, his eyes
searching patiently for sign of Golden Hawk. The
nights were colder and he was now fighting dis-
couragement. But he was nothing if not persistent.

Due to the constant presence of the mountain
lion—Weasel Piss had sighted him almost daily—
Weasel Piss did not remain at his lookout during
the night, and had retreated to the cabin, a necessity he hated. The place stank of Golden Hawk.

He rubbed his eyes, his heart suddenly thudding in his breast.

For so long he had waited for this moment,
when it came, he found it difficult to believe.
But there was no mistaking what he saw. A lone
rider—Golden Hawk—was breaking out of the
timber far below him, riding up the sloping
meadow toward his cabin.

For a long, delicious moment Weasel Piss
watched his quarry ride up the slope; then he
snatched up his bow, slung his quiver over his
back, and ducked into the brush to head back
down to the cabin before Golden Hawk reached
it. He had practiced this in his mind many times,
and he knew just how much time he needed to
reach the cabin in time.

He was running down the well-worn path his
moccasins had beaten into the grass when he

pulled up in consternation. Crouching on a rock over the trail, waiting for him to pass under, was the mountain lion. Terrified, Weasel Piss pulled up. It was almost as if the animal were in league with Golden Hawk, and yet he could not believe this—he would not.

Swiftly, he fitted an arrow to his bow and drew it back. Before he could let the arrow fly, the big cat lowered his head, pulled back, and vanished into a patch of brush above the trail. Trembling slightly, Weasel Piss slowly lowered his bow and waited for the animal to reappear farther down the trail, or perhaps move about and come at him from behind.

He whirled, his heart thudding, and caught a movement in the brush above him beside the trail, a tawny shape moving swiftly under a big cat's whiskered face, the enormous eyes a pale, luminous green. A chill ran up his spine. It was a devil cat for sure.

Slowly, his heart still pounding in this throat, Weasel Piss moved on down the trail, passing under the rock upon which the great cat had crouched a moment before. Once he was safely past it, he continued on down to the flat with renewed urgency, but when he reached it, he saw that Golden Hawk, astride his pony, was now in sight of the cabin. His plan—to wait calmly inside the cabin for his unsuspecting quarry to enter—was now impossible. That devil cat's sudden appearance had been enough to prevent him from reaching the cabin undetected.

He would wait until Golden Hawk entered the cabin and come at him from behind. He would bury an arrow in his back and then another in his chest if he turned to see who it was. It would not be very brave to kill the famed Golden Hawk in such a manner, but by now all Weasel Piss wanted was to strike down the hated Golden Hawk and return to his village with his golden hair as a trophy.

He waited until Golden Hawk dismounted and entered the cabin before he put his head down and darted up the slope, keeping the barn between him and the cabin.

Hawk called Raven Eyes again, but this time without much hope of a response. She would have answered the first time if she had been anywhere around. And from the look of the place, he knew she had not been there since he left. Frowning, he pulled up. He could smell Comanche. Then he caught sight of the blanket on the floor in a corner. The untidy fireplace. The scraps of meat on the floor. The untidiness overall, the sense that whoever was using his cabin did not live easily under a roof.

He darted to a window and was in time to see a Comanche brave vanish behind the barn. He was not fleeing, however. He was running toward the cabin, using the barn to keep himself hidden. It was only pure luck that Hawk had been able to catch that single glimpse of him.

He had recognized him at once: Weasel Piss.

He checked the load in his Colt and then the percussion cap on his Hawken. A moment later he left the cabin on the run and headed for the barn. He was almost to it when Weasel Piss appeared in the open doorway and let fly with an arrow. The arrow caught him in the left shoul-

der and sliced on through, the impact like that of
a tearing fist.

Sprawling forward onto the ground, Hawk fired
up at the Comanche with his Colt. Weasel Piss
staggered back as a tiny hole appeared in his left
thigh. Before Hawk could get off a second shot,
the Indian ducked back inside the barn. Hawk
kept his cocked revolver on the doorway, waiting
to see if the Comanche would try to cut him
down again. Nothing. He lay down the Colt and
inspected the arrow protruding from his shoulder. It was clear what he had to do, so he did it.
He snapped off the rear of the shaft, then gritted
his teeth and pulled the arrow on through his
shoulder; the pain when it grated past bone excruciating, but not disabling.

He realized he would not be able to use his
rifle. Leaving it in the grass, he kept his Colt in
his right hand and charged through the open
doorway into the barn. Bloody footprints led to
the windowsill. Glancing through the shattered,
sashless window, he saw Weasel Piss's tracks
heading for the timbered slope beyond the flat.
Doing his best to ignore the throbbing hell in his
left shoulder, Hawk stepped out through the window and trotted across the flat after the fleeing
Comanche. He had no difficulty at all following
him up through the timber. Weasel Piss was
losing considerable blood and was making no effort to cover his tracks.

It was close to sunset when he came out near
the cliff where Raven Eyes had been taken by
the mountain lion. The Comanche had headed
straight for the pile of boulders at its base. Hawk
pulled up on the edge of the meadow fronting

the cliff, aware that from those rocks he would make an excellent target. But so would Weasel Piss if he showed himself. His Colt in his right hand, Hawk darted straight across the meadow, watching the rocks carefully in case the Indian showed himself.

He reached the rocks without drawing any fire from the wounded Comanche, found a bloody moccasin print on a ledge above him, and clambered up after his quarry.

Through a haze of pain Weasel Piss saw Golden Hawk race across the flat and vanish in the rocks below. He was lying flat on a rock ledge and had lost so much blood he was light-headed. He no longer had the strength to draw back his bowstring. All he could hope for now was to get close enough to Golden Hawk to drop on him from a rock and bury his knife into him. He compressed his lips and waited, his eyes on the rocky trail beneath him, red with his blood.

He heard the sound of soft, padded feet strike the ledge behind him. The heavy smell of mountain cat was suddenly overpowering. He flung himself around to see the cougar's great whiskered face inches from his. He felt the cat's searing, foul breath as his mouth yawned open and he lunged for Weasel Piss's spine. He made a desperate effort to slash at the animal with his knife and heard the blade clattering to the surface of the rock dimly through a sudden, shattering explosion of pain as he realized the cat's teeth were closing on his neck. He heard bones snap and he screamed, but the sound of it echoed only deep within his own skull.

As if he were standing off from a great distance, he saw and felt his body, hanging loosely from the cat's jaws, being hauled up the rocks toward a cave entrance in the cliffside. And then an odd thought occurred to him: was this the vision he had repeatedly starved himself for and waited so long to receive?

And then all such questions, all thought, vanished into a great dark void.

When Hawk reached the ledge where Weasel Piss had lain in wait for him, and saw the explosion of blood, the clear imprint of the cat's paws in the blood, he knew what had happened as clearly as if the action were still taking place in front of him. He shuddered involuntarily. He had no love for this Comanche, but he felt sorry for him, nevertheless.

He knew also that it was time for him to track his cougar to his lair. He would never get a better opportunity, and this attack on the Comanche was proof, if any further proof were needed, that the cat was a hunter of men.

He was panting—as much from his own wound as from the climb—when he saw before him the cave entrance. Holding his Colt in front of him already cocked, he crouched low and continued up the long face of rock to the cave and peered in. The smell was unmistakably that of a wild animal's lair—compounded as it was of putrid, decaying flesh and the peculiar, acrid stench of moldering bone.

He moved in cautiously, and once his eyes were accustomed to the gloom, he was able to make out the sprawled, lifeless body of the

Comanche. But the cat was not in the cave that he could see. Under his buckskin shirt, a cold bead of sweat moved down his spinal column, chilling him.

He backed out of the cave and stood up. The sun perched on a long shelf of rock level with his eyes, and he could not see beyond it. Was the damned cat crouched there now, gathering his legs under him? He squinteed and waited for the sun to fall below the rim.

"Behind you," Raven Eyes cried as if she were standing only inches behind him.

Whirling, Hawk flung up his Colt. The cat was already in the air. His front paws slammed into Hawk's chest at the same time his Colt detonated. The force of the mountain lion's charge slammed Hawk backward to the caprock, and only dimly was he aware of cocking the Colt and firing a second round deep into the cougar's belly.

He lay there for a moment, dazed, the weight of the cat pressing upon him, his massive head resting almost lovingly across his right shoulder. Then, frantic suddenly, Hawk pulled himself out from under the dead animal and scrambled to his feet.

"Raven Eyes," he cried. "Where are you?"

But there was no answer. Only his echo. Again he called out to her, his eyes searching the flat below and the line of timber beyond. No response came, however, and after a few moments Hawk realized that none would be forthcomng.

Her warning cry to him had been only his imagination—or had it?

He went down on one knee to examine the mountain lion. In his prime he must have been a handsome animal. As it was, despite his wounds and age, he was still an awesome size. Hawk pulled the dead animal over and saw that his second shot had severed the animal's spine. The first shot would have been sufficient, however. The round had blown a hole in the cat's heart, the bullet then ranging down through his gut.

Hawk stood up and looked back into the cave where the dead Comanche lay and decided to leave him—and this great cat—for the wolves and coyotes. Then slowly and very carefully, for he was so weak he was shaking, he started to clamber down the rocks. As soon as he was able to travel, he would go to Raven Eyes' village and take her into his arms.

He tried not to hear the frightened, fear-laden voice sounding deep within him.

He stood beneath the burial scaffold where Raven Eyes' bound body had been placed only a week before. Beneath the scaffold, placed neatly on the ground, were her favorite bowls and cooking utensils and a tuft of wild flowers as delicate a blue as he could imagine. It was the sight of those freshly picked flowers that tore at him suddenly, causing his eyes to sting, his vision to blur.

Beside Hawk stood Raven Eyes' sister, Morning Star. Raven Eyes' father would not accompany Hawk to this sad place. Though it was not customary for a Crow warrior to show such sorrow for a woman—even his favorite daughter—he was inconsolable and would only sit silently in his lodge, smoking his pipe and nodding his head over and over to assuage his grief.

"When did she die?" Hawk asked Morning Star.

"A week ago."

"Which day?"

She looked at him in some surprise that this should be so important to him, and told him.

"And was it late in the day?"

"Yes."

"The sun was going down?"

She frowned at him and nodded. "Yes."

He looked back up at the securely wrapped body. Someday the scaffold would crumble and the body inside that heavy blanket would be scattered to the winds, and Raven Eyes would be free to return to that from which she came.

"That was when she came to me—when the sun was going down. She came to warn me, to save me."

"That is strange, what you say."

"No," Hawk told her. "Not for Raven Eyes."

He turned away from the scaffold, caught the reins of his horse, and swung into his saddle. With only a nod to Morning Star, he turned his mount and rode on down the hill.

He did not look back. He could not.

As Hawk backed out of the cabin, dribbling the remains of the coal oil after him, he heard the sound of hooves on the meadow behind him. Glancing back, he saw Buffalo Jim and Tames Horses riding up the slope toward him. He tossed the jug aside and turned to wait for them.

"We heard," Jim told him.

"We come to take you with us to this fine

valley," Tames Horses said. "It is not good for a man to grieve alone."

"What're you doin', hoss?" Jim asked, glancing down at the dark stream leading from the cabin and then over at the overturned jug resting on the ground.

"Getting set to leave."

Hawk turned, struck a sulfur match, and dropped it onto the trail of coal oil. The flame sputtered across the ground, exploded into the cabin, and a moment later the entire structure was pulsing with flames, black smoke billowing out the blown windows and open doorway.

"It smelled of Comanche," Hawk told them, starting toward his horse and the loaded packhorse on the lead beside it. "Where'd you say this valley of yours was, chief?"

Tames Horses booted his pony alongside Hawk and looked down at him, his face like old, warm sunlight. "I did not say. But this is big country. We will find it."

Hawk nodded. That was good enough for him.